Prophetess –
Psalms of the Damsel

CHARLES M STIRLEY

WESTBOW
PRESS®
A DIVISION OF THOMAS NELSON
& ZONDERVAN

WestBow Press books may be ordered through booksellers or by contacting:

WestBow Press
A Division of Thomas Nelson & Zondervan
1663 Liberty Drive
Bloomington, IN 47403
www.westbowpress.com
844-714-3454

Scriptures taken from the Holy Bible, New International Version®, NIV®.
Copyright © 1973, 1978, 1984, 2011 by Biblica, Inc.™ Used by permission
of Zondervan. All rights reserved worldwide. www.zondervan.com
The "NIV" and "New International Version" are trademarks registered
in the United States Patent and Trademark Office by Biblica, Inc.®

ISBN: 978-1-6642-7434-1 (sc)
ISBN: 978-1-6642-7435-8 (hc)
ISBN: 978-1-6642-7433-4 (e)

Library of Congress Control Number: 2022914058

Print information available on the last page.

WestBow Press rev. date: 9/27/2022

Contents

Prologue

Rephalah stood at the cauldron, cooking her meal. The kitchen hut was the largest of the chief's other huts. As she cooked, the spicy aroma went up through the thatched roof. As Rephalah cooked her mind wondered for a moment.

"Rephalah," said Kaleigh, the old maidservant that was helping her cook. "You need to concentrate."

"I'm sorry, Kaleigh. I just have a lot on my mind."

"Tell me, Rephalah. What is troubling you?"

"Kaleigh. I have a question: Do you think I'm beautiful?"

"Why of course. You are *still* an attractive woman."

"But how attractive do you think I am? You can be honest."

"I know my eyes are getting dimmer each day, but you still are a beautiful woman."

Rephalah laughed.

"Kaleigh you, really are going blind. Why do you lie?"

"I … was being honest."

"But tell me. Would you say that any man would still find me attractive?"

"Rephalah, you seemed very obsessed over this."

"You did not say yes, so I take it as a no."

Kaleigh sighed and put her hand on Rephalah's shoulder.

"Getting older is not easy, is it, Rephalah?"

"No, it's not. Especially when you have to worry about competing with another woman."

"Rephalah, believe me, I understand your struggle. It is something that all we women must deal with at some point."

"But I am not ready to do so, Kaleigh. Not now. What hope do I have now? How can he love me now? There is now a new woman in his life."

"Rephalah."

"I don't want to think about it now! Dinner is almost prepared. Go get my husband."

Kaleigh was about to go find the chief but he walked into the room. He was a big, hairy, barrel chested man. His long, dark beard covered his chest. He wore a robe of soft material; it was of fairly high quality.

"Did you finish dinner, Rephalah?" he said.

"Yes, milord. It is just about ready."

"Good. It has a nice aroma."

The chief went to the cauldron and smelled the stew.

"I cannot wait until dinner time."

Rephalah smiled.

Well at least, he appreciates my cooking still.

"I am glad it pleases you."

"I am so excited, Rephalah. Eleigh just told me she has a special surprise for me. She is going to show it to me during dinner."

And that just killed the mood. Eleigh! The other woman.

Oh, how I despise hearing that name.

"Rephalah, Kaleigh. Go prepare the supper. We are going to have a feast."

The king walked off joyfully. Rephalah put down the spoon and simply stood stiff.

"Are you alright, milady," said Kaleigh.

"No! Not in the slightest. How, Kaleigh! How could he do this to me! How could he take another wife?"

"Come now Rephalah. You've been through this before."

"Yes, but this time, I don't think I will be able to outlive this one. I just can't handle this anymore."

"Rephalah, you must be strong."

"I am trying but what strength I have is gradually fading."

Kaleigh held Rephalah's hand.

"I know you feel as though the gods have not been good to you. But believe me, your fortune can always change."

"At my age, I am well past the point of hope. Now come on. We have a dinner to prepare."

♪ ♪ ♭

Rephalah sat at the table in the dining hall with the chief and Eleigh. It was a medium sized table. The chief sat at the head of the table, and the two women sat across from each other. Rephalah often resisted trying to sit with the other woman but the chief wanted it. There was silence for a while.

"Milord," said Eleigh. "I have something for you."

Eleigh got up and called one of her maidservants. The servant came with a large cloak. The chief opened his mouth in oak. The cloak was quite lovely with beautiful blue dye, and the material was soft.

"Eleigh," said the chief. "Where did you get this?"

"Do not worry about that, milord. Let me put it on you."

The chief got up and Eleigh with the help of her servant put the cloak on the chief.

"Now you look like a true ruler."

"Thank you, Eleigh. Truly you are a blessing of the gods."

The chief gave Eleigh a kiss. Eleigh flashed Rephalah a victorious smile.

"Eleigh," said the chief. "This is the best gift that you could've given me."

"Well …" said Eleigh. "I wouldn't say that …"

"What are you saying?"

Eleigh touched her belly.

"You can't be serious."

"I am, milord."

The chief smiled and hugged Eleigh. Rephalah stood stiff as she watched the two hugged.

I cannot believe it!

"At last!" said the king. "I am going to be a father! Will it be a son?"

"It is possible. Let us hope to the gods that it is so. I know you have wanted one for a long time."

"Eleigh. Truly you have brought happiness into my life. I could not have asked for more."

Rephalah looked at the chief's smile. She thought back to a time when she herself used to make the chief smile like that. She looked at Eleigh. She had a glow on her face.

I remember when I glowed like that.

Rephalah wiped her eyes and stood up.

"I ask your permission to leave, milord."

"Yes, that is fine," the chief said nonchalantly.

Rephalah rushed out of the room. Kaleigh followed behind her.

♪ ♪ ♭

Rephalah was her in room crying. Kaleigh was comforting her.

"Please milady, be strong," said Kaleigh.

"But how? My own husband no longer loves me. His heart now belongs to someone else."

"Milady …"

"Kaleigh, I just don't think I can be here anymore."

"You want to leave? But you have a good life here!"

"But why stay? That woman is able to give the chief the one thing I could not! And am I becoming old. My beauty has faded."

"But milady, you are still an attractive woman."

"Says who? Kaleigh. Can you compare me to that other woman and say that I am more beautiful than her."

Kaleigh was silent.

"That's what I thought. What is the point of staying here. It would be far better for me to live in the wilderness of Enel, than to live here."

"Rephalah. Let's take a walk. Perhaps a little time alone with help you think about things."

"Okay," said Rephalah. "But I want to leave the village for a while."

"Milady ..."

"Just for a while, Kaleigh."

"But do you think the chief will allow that?"

"He is busy with his new wife. I might as well be dead to him. Let's go."

Kaleigh nodded.

♪ ♪ ♭

The two were at the village gate. The person who was standing guard looked at the two. He was a burly young man.

"Chieftess," said the guard. "Why are you here."

"I am just leaving on official business. I will return shortly."

"Is your husband okay with this," he said.

"Would I be here if he wasn't."

"I-I understand. Pardon my behavior."

He opened the gate.

"Be safe, chieftess."

"Thank you."

♪ ♪ ♭

Perhaps a little fresh air was all that was needed. The spring air was cool and the quiet allowed one to have plenty of time to think.

"Thank you, Kaleigh for walking with me," said Rephalah.

"Think nothing of it, milady. I have been with you sense you were born. I will always here for you."

"Kaleigh," said Rephalah. "When we are alone you can just call me Rephalah. I told you that."

"I know," said Kaleigh. "But in many ways I still see that majestic young lady from so long ago."

"That time has passed, Kaleigh. I remember, the time when I was loved by those around me. But now that is over. Sure I have some respect as chieftess, but the admiration and attention I once received is no longer there."

Kaleigh held her master's' hands.

"Mila-Rephalah. Moving on is difficult. I understand that this a difficult time for you. Believe me, I have experienced this time as well. But I want you to know that you are not alone."

Rephalah smiled.

"Thank you, Kaleigh. That means a lot to me."

Rephalah looked at the village.

"I have had a lot of memories there."

"Are you really thinking about leaving?"

"It may be for the better. There is no place for me there. The chief now has a new wife. One that is younger and beautiful. I would rather live somewhere else than be just another wife of the chief."

"Whatever, you decide," said Kaleigh. "I support your decision."

"Thank you, Kaleigh. You are a true friend."

Rephalah at that moment took out her flute and began to play. It was generally something that she did whenever she felt depressed. Music was a good way to cheer up. While she was playing, she heard someone sing.

You are my God. You envelope me in Your arms. In your hands I rest, and in your hands you keep me.

"What is that song," said Rephalah. "It is quite lovely."

"I am not sure," said Kaleigh.

The song became louder as they saw two women walking together. One was a young redhead with green eyes, and they other a pale, skinny woman with dark-hair. The redhead played the harp as she sung with the pale woman.

As Rephalah listened to the music all of a sudden her mind was at ease. She listened some more.

or you created my inmost being;
you knit me together in my mother's womb.
I praise you because I am fearfully and wonderfully made;
your works are wonderful,
I know that full well.
My frame was not hidden from you
when I was made in the secret place,
when I was woven together in the depths of the earth.
Your eyes saw my unformed body;
all the days ordained for me were written in your book
before one of them came to be.
How precious to me are your thoughts,[a] God!
How vast is the sum of them!

Were I to count them,
they would outnumber the grains of sand—
when I awake, I am still with you.(Psalms 139:13-
18 NIV)

It was as though all of Rephalah's stress was being melted away.

"This music," said Rephalah. "It is not like anything I heard before."

She walked up to the two women.

"Tell me," she said. "What is that music you are singing?"

"It is a song to our Lord," said Muchara. "We sing to Him."

"Ah, so that is your god?" said Rephalah. "Is he your favorite or your most powerful god?"

"He the ONLY god!" said the redhead. "He is our Friend and Protector. We love to sing songs of adoration to Him!"

The redhead grabbed the hand of Rephalah, with the harp still in her hand.

"Tell me what is your name?" she said.

"I am Rephalah. And yours."

"Call me Afeyna."

She clasped hands with Rephalah.

"A pleasure to meet you."

Afeyna seemed to be outgoing. Her face glowed with a lovely smile and there a happy expression in her green eyes. The pale one noticed the golden bracelet on Rephalah's hand.

"Tell me," she said. "Are you the wife of a chief? Or are you the leader of a village?"

"That village you see over there? That is my village. I am a wife of a chief. My name is chieftess Rephalah of the Ebry clan. This is my maidservant Kaleigh."

"A pleasure," said Kaleigh.

"But what are you doing out here," said the pale woman. "It is not often I see a chieftesses wandering alone outside their village."

"Sadly," said Rephalah. "I just don't think I can go back there. The chief has found another with whom to be happy."

"He has another wife!" said Afeyna.

Afeyna quickly embraced Rephalah.

"I am so sorry to hear that. Believe me, I understand your situation."

"How can you possibly understand? It is not like you understand my situa-"

Afeyna frowned.

"Actually I do. Believe me. I have been bitter about it a long time."

"But-" said Rephalah. "How could you understand. You are a very beautiful young woman. Why would husband love someone more than you."

"Beauty allows a woman to do many things. Sadly it does not allow one to bear children."

Rephalah was silent. Afeyna did not need to say anymore; that sentence was enough.

"So," said Rephalah. "I guest Kaleigh was right. I really am I not alone."

"I am so happy that we met," said Afeyna. "This meeting just had to be ordained by God!"

"Slow down!" said Rephalah. "Exactly what are you talking about? What exactly do you mean when you say 'ordained?'"

"What Afeyna was saying," said the pale woman in a calm tone of voice. "is that this meeting is no coincidence. The Lord God has made it so we would have this meeting."

Rephalah looked at the two a little confused.

"Are you saying that this God of yours led me to come out here so that we could meet?"

"Yes!" said Afeyna.

"So this God of yours can do things like that?"

"He can do many things," said the woman. "That is not even a fraction of it."

"Well when I heard your song, I did feel bit comforted. When you two came with your singing, my heart felt more at ease."

"That is the power of our God," said the woman. "When you came here to contemplate and to mourn. He sent us to give you healing. I know you have experienced difficulties. Losing a child is not easy and finding out that the other woman is with child is a lot to bear."

"How did you know that?" said Rephalah. "I did not tell you that."

"My God can reveal many things to His servants," she said with a smile.

"Just who are you?"

"My name is Muchara."

"Your accent sounds a bit heavy. Tell me are you from the Northern part of Illunra?"

"Yes, I came from that wilderness of Enali."

"Wow! You actually lived there? How do you survive over there."

"The Enels are a tough people. We know the area very well. And there are plenty of animals available for hunting."

"What brings you over here?"

"I was led by God to come here. My mission is to bring to spread the good news all throughout this island."

"The good news?" said Rephalah. "What is that?"

"That is what I am going to talk to you about." Muchara said with a smile.

"I am listening," said Rephalah.

Chapter 1

In many ways Rephalah saw herself in that beautiful redhead with the forest green eyes and the voice of the wood spirits. In her green tunic and plaid skirt she almost looked like a fairy that emerged from the forests of Clehria. As Afeyna,the redhead damsel stood surrounded by the attentive village, Rephalah was in many ways reminded of her on youth. The sight of this beauty stirred both admiration and jealously.

If I only could be young again

Rephalah was playing her flute to Afeyna's singing. All the villagers seemed immersed in the lyrics that Afeyna sung. The song was reacted to in different ways: Some prayed. Some stood up and sung loudly and others seemed to cry.

As Rephalah herself was playing. her worries seemed to be washed away by a peace that was coming over her. Afeyna did not even seemed to matter now as something inside of Rephalah was calling her to look to Someone higher.

Okay, Lord. I'm looking to you.

Muchara, the slim, pale woman with dark hair, in a burlap robe, was standing next to Afeyna singing alongside her. But often she is overshadowed by Afeyna's enchanted voice. Muchara however by the look on her face did not seem to mind. She was just enjoying the singing.

Rephalah felt a strong, warm, sensation coming over her. As

1

Rephalah felt something pressing over her heart, she almost fell to the ground. Being wrapped in this warm, burning sensation, the world around her did not seem to matter anymore. It was as though something was pressing against her heart.

Okay Lord, I am here.

While Rephalah was in this sensation, it was as though hours were going by; time did not seem to matter. She heard the monks and the villagers in the crowd all singing together, moved. It was obvious that God is moving.

Even as the song was ending the sensation remained. At the conclusion of the song ended the Abbot Keith walked in the middle of the crowd and said with a deep, manly voice.

"I feel the presence of God here."

Abbot Keith is a big, man so his frame gave him an imposing presence. He began to preach. He preached the Biblical story until he came to the conclusion.

"That is why the Lord God has came in the form of man in order to save you. If any of you feel God speaking to your heart. Come and receive him."

Rephalah smiled as she saw some of the people come to the Abbot. Abbot Keith began to pray for each and everyone of them. Rephalah herself began to cry and she the joy that many of them began to have.

Truly You are a Great God.

The joy on the people's faces reminded Rephalah of she first became a Christian herself.

♪ ♪ ♭

After service the monks were serving food in the village. There was a roasted pig suspended over the pit. Rephalah and Afeyna were talking as they drank a bit of water.

"That was a really good service," said Rephalah. "I felt blessed during that service. I really feel renewed."

"So do I," said Afeyna.

As they talked a lot of villagers went up to Afeyna and Rephalah.

"That was great singing," they said.

"Thank you," said Afeyna. "I am glad that you enjoyed it."

"You truly are a great bard," said a villager.

"I cannot take take credit for it. It the Lord God that blessed me to be able to sing that way."

"Truly you are blessed by that God."

Afeyna chuckled.

"Thank you. But I also had the help of Rephalah."

Although Rephlah received a complement from Afeyna, apparently to the villagers it seemed irrelevant as they kept talking to Afeyna. Really it was as if Rephalah was not even there. Rephalah sighed.

Why do I even bother to travel with you, Afeyna?

Rephlah walked away.

"Where are you going, Rephalah," said Afeyna.

"To get something to eat. I will meet up with you later."

While Rephalah was walking away, Mucara, a pale, slim woman with dark hair, saw her.

"Rephalah," said Muchara. "Are you okay. You seem upset."

"It's nothing, Muchara. I am fine."

"We've traveled together for a long time, Rephalah," said Muchara. "I know you well. You are not very good at hiding your emotions."

Rephalah sighed.

"Yeah, I suppose you're right."

"It's just that …"

3

"Afeyna ..."

They both said it at the same time.

"I know you, Rephalah."

Rephalah looked over at Afeyna, who was still talking with the crowd. Rephalah sighed.

"You know in many ways, I do see myself in Afeyna. She reminds me a lot about myself."

"Is it Afeyna that you see, or is it Eleigh?"

"I would say a little bit of both," said Rephalah. "Either way, I did share something in common with them at one time."

Muchara put her arm around Rephalah.

"I know the past at times can hurt. But one must move on," said Muchara. "The Lord has something better for you."

"I believe it, but still. Sometimes I want to go back. Back to a time when I used to receive much love."

"But, Rephalah. Isn't the love you receive from your Heavenly Father not enough?"

"Of course it is!" said Rephalah. "He saved me. He restored me. He made me feel whole again."

"Yet you act as though the reverse is true."

Repahalah was quiet for a moment.

"Yes, you do have a point. It's just that ... Muchara. It does hurt at times."

"I know. But you do have your Heavenly Father to talk to. You can always bring your concerns to him."

"I know."

"Be encouraged Rephalah. Be encouraged."

"Indeed," said a deep bellowing voice. "We must encourage one another in this walk. It can be difficult, but we must stay focused."

It was Abbot Keith.

"Abbot Keith," said Muchara with a smile. "You can be

such a nosy person at times. It's rather rude to come in on a private conversation."

"My apologies," said Abbot Keith a chuckle. "I always interested hear the gossip of women."

"Abbot!" said Rephalah. "Weren't you just listening?"

"I heard Rephalah, I heard. I was only joking."

The Abbot was a big man with a few gray hairs on his head. His face was fat and a little babyish. His appearance did in fact make him look like a big giant, baby. Rephalah almost laughed when she saw his appearance.

"Rephalah, do not be saddened. God has a purpose for all."

"Yes," said Rephalah. "But some have a greater purpose than others."

"But sometimes those with a greater purpose needs those with a smaller purpose. A king rules, be still needs servants. A general still needs soldiers."

Rephalah sighed.

"So I am just a good as a servant, am I. That's good to know. I guess I must serve Queen Afeyna."

"Rephalah," said the abbot. "Queen or servant all must serve God."

"I need to be alone."

Rephalah walked off leaving Muchara with the Abbot.

"Muchara," said Abbot Keith. "Rephalah has seemed very troubled recently."

"Rephalah is just a little bit stuck in the past," said Muchara. "But one day she will learn to move on."

"Aren't you going to talk with her," said the abbot.

"I will let her have a little time alone."

"I understand."

Abbot Keith looked at Afeyna for a moment. The girl was talking to the crowd of people.

"Afeyna has a beautiful voice. And she is such a beautiful soul," said the Abbot.

"And body as well," said Muchara.

The Abbot laughed.

"Indeed. She is becoming quite popular. Every village we visit have received her well."

"Mostly the men. The women in the villages don't seem to think the same way."

"Muchara," said the Abbot as he put his hand on Muchara's shoulder. "Please be with Rephalah and Afeyna. They need you."

"You think so?"

"I know so. I feel that God has something great in store for Illunra, but many wish to hinder it. Of course God is not limited by people. Neverthless I do believe that he wants us to do our part."

"And Afeyna has a great big part in that?"

"Yes. She may probably face some difficult times. You may not feel it now but there is always a problem before the provision. God according to Scripture has made significant promises to his people, but those people often had to be tested. We see this king David and Abraham."

"And Rephalah. What of her?"

"I feel that she too will have a role that she must play."

"I and my part is to prepare them."

Abbot Keith nodded.

"You understand well. You are quite wise."

"Well, I have learned from you and the monks. But tell me Abbot Keith was is your part?"

Abbot Keith gave Muchara a sly smile.

"You'll find out soon."

Afeyna ran up to the two calling out to them.

"Muchara! Abbot! Food's ready."

"I am not really hungry," said Muchara.

"Why not?"

"I just can't stop thinking about what Abbot Keith said about the part he plays in God's vision for Illunra."

Muchara smiled slyly at St. Keith.

"Perhaps it can wait after dinner."

"Wait!" said Afeyna. "Now *I* am curious. Tell us, St. Keith!"

"Do you trust me?"

"Of course! Why would ask that," said Abbot. Keith.

"If you would let me lead. Then I will take you to where I feel God wants me to go."

The abbot gave the two a sly smile.

"Abbot Keith," said Muchara. "Why are you always playing games. Really I don't know what to make of this."

"Muchara," said Abbot Keith. "Whenever God leads a person, very often that person is not sure of where God is taking him. At times he even has a bit of fear. But that person continues on, trusting God."

"I have a feeling that I know where this is going," said Muchara.

St. Keith put his hand on Muchara's shoulder.

"Muchara, I am excited for where God wants to take Illunra. And I have a feeling that you are too."

"Indeed. You have waited a long time for an 'awakening.'"

"And can't you feel it," said the Abbot.

"Yes, Abbot," said Muchara. "I can."

"I certain can!" said Afeyna. "I feel excited"

"So Abbot, where are you taking us?"

"I just ask that you trust me," said the Abbot. "I have been praying about this for a very long time. I have fasted many nights and I feel that this where God wants me to go."

Afeyna and Muchara looked at each other.

"If you truly feel lead to do this," said Muchara. "Then we trust your judgment. We will follow if this is direction from God."

"I am ready as well!" said Afeyna. "This is something big! I feel it! I am so excited!"

Abbot Keith smiled.

"Thank you both. Your support means much to me."

Chapter 2

Afeyna as she was walking with St. Keith and the group of monks to the next village, she thought about what St. Keith told about this new destination.

Where could he be taking us.

Afeyna has been thinking about this new destination for a while now and she kept asking Abbot Keith where it was he was taking them.

"You will find out," he simply kept saying.

Afeyna did not know the region of Rolunda very well so she could only guess what the place could. As she approached a large white castle, she soon found that she would not have to guess anymore. Abbot Keith gave Afeyna a big smile.

"Have you figured it out now?"

Afeyna laughed.

"Really, Abbot Keith, you are something."

Abbot Keith chuckled.

"No, in reality, I am *nobody*. I am just *somebody* who loves to serve the Lord."

"This is very impressive," said Rephalah.

"Yes, it is."

"Abbot!" said Muchara. "Why did you bring us here?"

"I know it may see odd to you, Muchara, but in my heart, I felt led to come here."

"Do you know where you have brought us?"

"Of course. To the king's castle."

Muchara sighed.

"Really St. Keith, I am not sure what to say about all this."

"Believe me, Muchara. I have struggled with this as well. But I have prayed and prayed and really, this is where I feel we need to be."

Afeyna took Muchara by the hand.

"Muchara, I know it feels like a big jump but lets move in faith. In many ways I feel led to be here."

Muchara looked at Afeyna with silence.

"What's wrong, Muchara?"

"It's nothing, Afeyna."

"Do you really feel that is where we should be?"

"You don't feel the same way," said Afeyna.

"I just have a bad feeling ... that's all."

"If you do then please tell us."

"Yes," said St. Keith. "Is it nervousness. Do you feel like vomiting."

"You could say that," said Muchara.

"Muchara," said St. Keith. "If you don't feel right about this, I understand. I will not force you to come if you don't want to."

"No," said Muchara. "If this is were you believe God wants us to be then I will come with you."

"Are you sure," said St. Keith.

"Yes," said Muchara. "Let's go."

Afeyna held Muchara's hand.

"Then we go forward."

Rephalah looked at the castle herself. She herself had an uncomfortable feeling in her stomach.

"I do understand why Muchara feels the way she does. I am a chief wife and I myself have never visited a place like this."

"Neither have I," said St. Keith. "That is why we step out in faith together."

Afeyna nodded.

"Exactly now let's go."

Afeyna instantly walked ahead of everyone. Rephalah looked at Afeyna's face.

That glow. In many ways I was like that when I was young.

"We are coming Afeyna," said Rephalah.

Rephalah looked back at everyone else.

"Are we going or not."

St. Keith chuckled.

"I love your attitude," he said. "Come everyone. Let's make haste."

♪ ♪ ♭

Two watchmen looked atop the castle. They saw a group of people walking toward the castle.

"Look," said one of them. "It looks like we have travelers."

"Yes," said the second watchmen. "I wonder what they could possibly want."

"Do you think they are messemgers of war?"

"I don't see any horses or chariots. They are all on foot. That doesn't seem like something a messenger of war would to."

"You think we should tell the king?"

"Yes, that seems like a good idea."

♪ ♪ ♭

"What a beautiful castle!"

"Yes, it's quite a wonder."

11

Rephalah and Afeyna looked at the large, marble, white castle with its many turrets and its large entrance looking at them like the mouth of a dragon ready to breath fire or engulf its prey as its large gate opened. The castle looked like a marvel from afar, but upclose it appeared to be even more grand.

"Yes," said St. Keith. "The castle was made from the marble found in the region of Enali."

"How were they even able to get that heavy marble over here," said Afeyna.

"Many claimed," said St. Keith, "That the giants of Enali helped bring some of it here a long time."

"So they are actually some good giants," said Afeyna. "In the sagas they were always portrayed as bad."

"They don't have to necessarily be giants," said Muchara. "In Enali, they are very tall people and they are quite strong. Together they would not have much problem bringing all this marble here."

As they stood outside, they saw one of the men looking a window.

"Strangers! For what reason do you come?"

"We have come to bear good tidings to the king," St. Keith, "Tidings of joy and peace."

"Oh, and what are these tidings you bear."

"They are tidings from our Lord Jesus Christ."

The two men looked at each other perplexed.

"Jesus?" said one of them. "I do not believe I have heard of that name. Is He a chief of your village."

"He is more then that. He is Lord of all and I would love to tell you more about Him."

The two men murmured among to each other. They were wondering if this fat, old man was either a maniac or a messenger that came from the mountains.

"Who exactly is this 'Jesus' you speak off," said the chief.

"If you allow us entry, we shall tell you more."

"Yes, please," said Afeyna. "If you allow us entry we will tell you all about you. He wants to have a meeting with not just the king, but everyone here. Please let us in and we will tell you all about our lord."

The men gave each other a skeptical look. However as they looked at Afeyna's beautiful face, it was hard to say no.

"If you give us a moment we will go talk to the king."

"Thank you," said Afeyna.

♪ ♪ ♭

"They want to talk with me about 'Jesus.' Who is he?" said the king.

"From what I gather he is a Great Lord."

The king seemed perplexed.

"This group. Did they come riding on chariots of gold with milk white stallions?"

"No they walked."

"Are they wearing gowns of the finest silk and decked with golden broaches and necklaces?"

"No they are wearing common robes."

"Then how is he a great lord when he sends such a minuscule group to greet me. Surely he would've come greeting me chariots and stallions at least."

"Well he apparently seem to have very beautiful servant girl."

"A servant girl? What is she like. She has wild, fiery hair and eyes that are as green as the forest. She wants to introduce you to her lord. She seems quite eager to share him with you."

The king sighed.

"This better not be a waste of my time. Let them in!"

♪ ♪ ♭

Rephalah stood waiting. She did shake a little. What is the king going to say? How will he receive this group? Rephalah looked at Afeyna. Afeyna just looked out into the distance. She did seem to fidget a little.

"How are you feeling about this, Afeyna?"

"I do feel a little bit nervous, Rephalah," said Afeyna. "But at the same time, I do feel a bit excited. This really could be a big opportunity for us."

"Yes!" said St. Keith. "You all must have faith."

"Favor or not," said Mark, "I am ready to die. I do not fear. I know God will be with us even at our deaths."

"That is the attitude," said St. Keith. "Have courage everyone. There is no need to be afraid."

The door the castle went up. When Afeyna viewed it was like watching the mouth of the dragon open. A group of men adorned in warrior garments and carrying banners came and welcomed them.

"Greetings travelers," said the leader of the group. "The king has accepted your offer to introduce him to your Lord."

"How wonderful!" said Afeyna.

"Come with us," said the guard.

The men let the group inside the castle. Rephalah looked at Kaleigh, her maidservant.

"Are you okay, Kaleigh? You have been quiet."

"I was just thinking, that's all. I never thought I would be here."

"Neither did I."

"And the the thought that the king would invite us here. I never thought I would live to see this day."

"Yes, the Lord is wonderful isn't he?"

"Yes, he does amaze me. But will he make the king deal kindly with us."

"We will find out. We just have to have faith."

"I will have have faith when I see for myself how the king deals with St.Keith."

"But, Kaleigh, to have faith is to believe even when you don't see or know what will happen. Besides, we made it this far didn't we?"

Kaleigh chuckled.

"Fine then, Rephalah. I suppose I can believe a little."

"Kaleigh," said St. Keith. "You are about to see the favor of the Lord at work"

Kaleigh looked at St. Keith with a silent blank stare.

Well I do admire his attitude.

St. Keith walked boldly in the front of the group. Kaleigh saw the confident look on his face.

He is either very confident or very foolish.

The men led the group to the door of the king's throne room. The leader nodded at the door's guards, and the door was opened, revealing the king. St. Keith and his friends were motioned to come forward. When Rephalah looked at the king he saw that he did have a lean physique and his scraggly beard and fierce expression showed that he was a warrior with a lot of experience.

"Welcome everyone," said the king.

St. Keith stepped forward.

"Greetings, sire. I am honored to meet your acquaintance."

"I have heard that you have come to bring good tidings."

"Yes," said St. Keith. "The Lord Jesus have sent us here to share the good news of His resurrection."

The king himself seemed perplexed.

"What are you babbling about?" said the king.

"I am here to tell you have of our Lord and Savior, the Jesus Christ."

"Who is he? Is a king or the chief of a tribe?"

"He is the king above all kings."

The king at that moment seemed a bit irritated.

"Stop wasting my time!" said the king. "I was gracious enough to invite you in my presence and yet you come babbling nonsense to me. You have one minute to say what you need to say. Otherwise I am going to put an end to this."

"Very well then. Perhaps Afeyna can explain it better."

Afeyna froze for a moment.

Abbot what are you thinking?

Abbot Keith motioned for Afeyna to come forward. Seeing Afeyna shake a little bit, Rephalah did feel bad for her. Afeyna clenched her wooden harp tightly. The king eyed Afeyna a little bit. Actually even the guards gave her a few interested looks. That did make Rephalah think back to her youth for moment.

I remember what that was like for me

Afeyna took out her harp and bowed for a moment.

"It is an honor to meet you, my king."

"What is your name, damsel?"

"I am Afeyna."

"Well then, Afeyna. What do you have to say to me. Are you going to babble on like this one here."

"Actually, my king," said Afeyna. "What I want to tell you. I would like to do it in song form."

Afeyna began playing.

In the beginning was the Word(John 1:1)

And from there began the story of Creation. Afeyna sung as though she was singing an epic saga. The creation of the world. Afeyna told a story of the Garden of Eden, and sung of the creation of Adam and his wife Eve.

Rephalah saw that the king was engrossed the story. Either that or it was Afeyna's beauty. Maybe it was both. Jealousy did sting Repalah's soft heart as she saw Afeyna receiving a longing stare. Rephalah clenched her garment tightly.

Oh if only that was me!

Rephalah almost wanted to leave the room after seeing Afeyna get some attention, but that would of course be disrespectful. She saw the king seemed invested in the story as Afeyna sung about the serpent that came into the garden tricking Adam and Eve into eating the forbidden fruit, immediately causing Adam and Eve to be separated from God.

Afeyna ended the song with the what the Lord told the serpent about the Word in Genesis(3:15):

A seed will come forth. He will bruise your head and you will bruise his heel.

Afeyna ended the song there.

"So what more happens?" said the king.

"If you want to know that," said Afeyna. "You will have to wait until the next day."

The king chuckled a bit.

"I must say, damsel. You are quite clever."

"Are you starting to understand a bit more." said Abbot Keith.

"Yes..a bit more."

"Okay then old man," said the king "you have piqued my interest. These 'sins' your Lord have died for. What exactly are they?"

"It is anything that is contrary to what God desires. Anything against his will."

The king gave St. Keith a blank stare.

"A long time ago there was a man named Adam. He is the father all humanity. God created him and put him in a garden. He was given only one command: Not to eat from a certain tree. He disobeyed and as a result of his disobedience, sin entered the world."

"Hmm ..." said the king. "Interesting. Well this story of yours is interesting ... if not a bit odd. I should expel you from my presence but this damsel here has sung very well."

"Thank you, milord," said Afeyna.

"Come here, damsel."

Afeyna gave Abbot Keith a stare. The abbot nodded at her. Afeyna walked up to the king.

"Don't be shy, damsel. Come closer."

Afeyna walked a bit closer. Afeyna saw the king examine her closely. The king put his hand on Afeyna's face. Afeyna found the king's hand to be firm but gentle.

"I must say, you are a beautiful young damsel."

"Thank you, my king."

"Tell me damsel. Would it interest you to stay a little longer. You are good singer. The chiefs here would be happy to have you at our banquet."

"I can, but may I ask you a favor?"

"Ask."

"If you would have me here, can my companions stay here as well?"

The king sighed.

"I suppose. This group while odd is interesting so I suppose they could stay here a little longer."

"Thank you my king."

At that moment a guard came up to him.

"My king, the queen requests your presence."

The king seemed alarmed for a moment.

"What for?"

"She just said it's for a an important matter."

"Very well. But guard. Take the group to their guest quarters."

"Yes my king."

As the guard led Afeyna and group to the door they passed by the Queen. The group froze for a moment when they saw her. The queen was tall, slender and beautiful, with ice blue eyes that gave a freezing stare. That glare seem liked it was aim specifically at Afeyna.

"Hello," said the queen "Are you all the travelers that came give your gifts to the king?"

"Yes, we have," said Abbot Keith. "And it is an honor to meet you my queen."

"Thank you, old man. So tell me you all came on behalf a king I heard."

"Yes, we have."

The queen examined the clothes of the abbot and the group.

"I must say, for a group of people who came representing a king you all sure have dressed humbly."

"The power of our Lord Jesus is very better than any silver or gold."

"Is that so? Well then I would like to meet this Jesus of yours soon."

"You can right now. He is not far from you. Just open your heart and ask Him to reveal himself to you, He will."

The queen sighed.

"I can meet Him later."

The queen looked at Afeyna. Afeyna froze for a moment at the queen's glare.

"I heard your singing, damsel. I must say, you have a very beautiful voice."

"Thank you my, queen," said Afeyna.

"So are you and your group going to be staying here for a while?"

"Yes ..." said Afeyna.

"Well then. All of you enjoy your stay here then."

The queen left them, but when she did looked at Muchara eye to eye. The queen paused for a second and then left and went to the king. Afeyna did feel a little bit of a chill when the queen passed her. Muchara put her hand on Afeyna's shoulder.

"Don't let her scare you," she whispered. "She loves to make people feel fear. That is how she controls people."

"Okay," said Afeyna.

The guard motioned for them to follow him. The group followed and were given a bit of tour of the castle. They were shown the rooms where the servants sleep and also were they kept the kitchen. They were then taken to their guest rooms.

The hallway had plenty of guest rooms. Each was able to have his own room.

"These rooms are so nice!" said Afeyna.

The rooms were nice and cozy, and the beds looks comfortable as well.

"You all should feel honored," said the guard. "Is not often that the king would share these rooms with such commoners."

"We are honored," said the abbot. "And it is our hope that the king himself will feel honored as well."

"Ha!" said the guard. "How could you possibly give honor to the king. Are you going to honor him with your 'Jesus.'"

"Believe me, my friend. To have Jesus is the highest honor that one can receive."

The guard shook his hand.

"Really I am not sure what to say to you. In some ways I see why the king decides to keep you around for a little bit longer. You are a little bit amusing."

The abbot gave the guard a serious stare.

"You may not be as aware of it," said the abbot. "But you yourself seek the light. You mock the light but in many ways you long for it."

The guard shook his hand.

"I heard enough of this. I'm out."

The guard looked at the rest of the group.

"Really," he said. "I don't know you deal with this guy. Unless you really believe this."

The guard left. Afeyna put her hand on St. Keith's arm.

"Don't let him bother you Abbot Keith."

"I doesn't bother me at all, I count it joy to be mocked for my Savior. Afeyna don't be afraid to show your light, okay."

"Okay, Abbot."

The abbot smiled at Afeyna. It was always great to see that smile on his face. Whenever he smiled, his face shined like the sun.

"Well then," said Kaleigh. "Since we are here, i guess we can take a rest."

"Kaleigh, you want to sleep already?"said Rephalah. The day is not even over yet."

"You know I am old, Rephalah. I am not like you all. I cannot be travelling all the time."

"Rest," said Abbot Keith. "You deserve it"

"Thank you, abbot. Now, I am going to rest. Wake me up when it's to eat."

♪ ♪ ♭

After having spoke with the king, Queen Ereigh decided to sit together with her servant Elsiu. in a second balcony of the second floor of the castle. They drank wine together as they enjoyed the fresh air, warm sunlight and bright clouds. The queen looked at her wine glass enjoying it.

"My queen, what do you think about the damsel," said Elsiu.

The queen played with her wine a little.

"What about her. She can be managed," said Queen Ereigh. " I don't think I will worry about Afeyna for a while. Tell me did you see the pale woman with dark hair and dressed in a robe?"

"Yes, I saw her from afar. She looked at bit strange. I can't really put my finger on it."

"Indeed. I will watch have to watch our guest."

Queen Ereigh examined the glass of wine.

"Do you plan on doing anything with them?"

"Not yet. I want to take a little more time to learn about them."

The queen sipped on the wine glass.

"And then after I've learned about them. I will deal with them in my own way."

Ereigh swallowed the rest of her wine and looked at the clear blue sky.

Chapter 3

"I never thought we would actually be here."

"St. Keith was right," said Rephalah. She shook her head. "I must admit that he truly is a man of faith."

"Yes!" said Afeyna. "I truly do admire him."

Afeyna sat in the room with Muchara and Rephalah, after having slept well.

"Yes" said Muchara. "But you yourself had a part it in. Your stepping and out and singing have brought you favor with the king."

"Indeed," said Rephalah. "It would appear that the king wants to keep you around. It must be great find such admiration."

"To be honest it makes me feel a little bit nervous," said Afeyna. "Really did you see the queen look at me? It would appear that she is jealousy."

Muchara nodded.

"Be careful of that woman, Afeyna. Something in me doesn't trust her."

"Yeah, that woman, does seem very cold," said Rephalah.

"Yes, I know!" said Afeyna. "Her stares make me shiver. I really don't feel comfortable around her."

"Afeyna," said Muchara. "Be careful that you don't get too

close to the king. I do believe you have caught his interest. And that can put you in danger. Be careful, Afeyna."

"Don't worry, Muchara," said Afeyna. "I will be fine. I dealt with jealous women before and if I can handle them I can handle the queen."

Rephalah looked at Afeyan critically and thought for a moment.

I'm sure you have Afeyna … I'm sure you have."

"And besides," Afeyna said as held her wooden harp. "The Lord is with me. Why should I fear a mortal woman."

"I like your attitude," said Muchara. "But also remember that you should watch *and* pray."

Afeyna hugged Muchara and said, "Don't worry, I will be fine. Also I have you by side."

"Yes, Afeyna, I am here."

Muchara hugged Afeyna.

"I am proud of you, Afeyna," said Muchara. "You have advanced far."

"It is because of your help, Muchara. And yours too, Rephalah."

"We are here for you, Afeyna," said Rephalah.

"I know."

There was a knock on the door. It was Abbot Keith overshadowing the three women with his large frame.

"Afeyna," said the Abbot. "The king would like to have an audience with you."

"Your clothes are prepared for you," said another voice.

It was one of the guards. He came to them with colorful decorated with golden trimmings.

"These robes were prepared by the queen for you," said the guard. "She does not want you presenting yourselves in such tattered clothing."

24

Afeyna looked at the garments. Wow they are so beautiful.

"Prepare yourselves for the visit," said the guard. "You can take your time. You don't want to look raggity for your visit."

♪ ♪ ♭

The three women left the room and a guard was there to lead them to the throne room. Though Afeyna already visited the king the day before, there was still a bit of nervousness at at the thought of seeing him again. He looked fierce but he did have a rugged handsomeness to him.

Rephalah looked at Afeyna. Afeyna looked happy,but why not? There seemed to be so much good happening to her. She has the admiration of many villagers, and of the Abbot and it would appear that the king himself is starting to take a liking to her.

Why can't I have that life.

Seeing Afeyna's popularity made her long to her youth back.

If only I could be young again.

The monks that were with them were talking among themselves. They were talking about their hopes for the future, and how they going to spread the Gospel. Muchara seemed a bit skeptical. The queen stood in front of the door with a young woman. Rephalah saw Afeyna freeze for a moment.

"Why do you look so alarmed?" said the Queen. "I am here to welcome you."

The queen looked the group. They looked much different in their color robes then when they were in their ragged clothes. Rephalah saw the young woman with look at Afeyna with a curious look. Was it that she was in awe of Afeyna's beauty or was it that she was just curious about her?

"Now you all looked well suited to see a king,"

25

♪ CHARLES M STIRLEY

"We really enjoy these clothes," said Afeyna. "We *feel* well suited to meet a king."

Rephalah saw the queen walk up to Afeyna. Afeyna's posture did stiffen a bit in the presence of the queen.

"Why are you so stiff, Afeyna. I know being before a king can be intimidating but relax. The king has taken a liking to you."

"I know. It still makes me feel a bit nervous."

"Don't worry," said the queen. "You will be fine."

The queen saw Afeyna's wooden harp.

"That harp ... Is it made from the oak of Clehria. It was a gift from a friend."

"From a friend? Who?"

"Muchara."

Then Rephalah looked at the queen but the queen looked over and saw Muchara. The two glanced at each other for a moment. The queen walked up to her for a moment.

"Is something wrong,..queen,"said Muchara.

"No ... it is not. It's just that you look familiar."

"How so?"

"I am sure.It's just that I feel that I might have seen you before. Tell me. Are you from this region."

"I come from Enali."

"Ah ... an Enel. I haven't seen one in a long time. Well you are tall, but you are a bit slender for an Enel."

"I guess you could say I don't eat as much as other Enels."

"Well whatever you eat, it sure haven't helped your complexion."

"Well perhaps that will change after eat at *your* table."

Ereigh chuckled.

"I like you, Enel. In some ways I am glad the king decided the keep you all around."

"And in other ways."

"The less said about that better. Now come. The king is waiting."

The queen led the group into the throne room where the king was sitting. Rephalah saw the king looking at Afeyna with wide eyes and a dropped jaw.

"I must say, Afeyna. Now you truly do look like you were sent by a king. And I suppose in some ways you are," the king said with a laugh.

"Yes, I was sent by a king," said Afeyna. "I was sent by Him to minister to you."

"Well then I must say, I am starting to like this king of yours," he said.

"My king," Ereigh said. "I do believe the group is wandering why they were sent."

"Really," said the king. "I was largely expecting Afeyna, but extra company is fine. Afeyna come here."

Rephalah saw the queen looking at Afeyna as she approached the king; the queen was not taking her eyes off the two. Rephalah's heart sank as she looked at Afeyna.

Poor Afeyna. In some ways I feel jealous. In others, I feel jealous.

"Well then," said the king. "I guess you will be finishing that song for me."

"I prefer to *continue* it."

The king laughed.

"Really, Afeyna. Do you plan to come here everyday."

"Whether I come here everyday or not, I will leave that you."

"Very well then, Afeyna. *Continue* your song."

Afeyna took out her wooden harp and began singing. She started to tell the story of Israel and how this would lead to the

promise of the seed. The song lasted a while and Afeyna ended
the song where the Word of God taking flesh.

The young woman looked at Afeyna with a dropped jaw,
the king looked at Afeyna with awe on his face, and the queen
was even more focused on Afeyna. By the look on Ereigh's face,
it was to tell if Ereigh was grimacing at her or is just focused
on Afeyna.

The king looked at Abbot Keith.

"Fat man," the king said to Abbot Keith. "You too come
here."

Abbot Keith came up to him.

"Is this girl the means by which you will share this Gospel?"

"I share the gospel by whichever way the Lord chooses. If
he chooses to use Afeyna to reveal His truth to you, that is fine.
But if He chooses just to have me speak to you to share the
Gospel that is fine as well. The main thing is that the Gospel
is shared."

"Well then I must say. Your Lord may have chosen the best
way to introduce me to it," the king said with a laugh. "Tell
me, Afeyna it would please you to come here everyday to come
sing to me would it."

"Why of course."

However, at that moment, an idea seemed to come to the
king.

"Actually …" said the king. "We do have a banquet coming
up in just a couple of weeks. Perhaps you could *continue* your
song their."

"Really?" said Afeyna.

"Yes. Well..actually … how would you like to *finish* your
song at the banquet."

"Are you sure," said Afeyna. "Two weeks is a long time."

"I can wait."

"I am not sure what to say," said Afeyna.

"I think you should do it," said the queen. "This is a great opportunity for you. Very few people in Rolunda have ever had the honor of playing before the king and his chief. I think you should."

"Wow, do you really mean it," said Afeyna.

"What do you think," said the queen. "If I didn't mean it do you think I would have said it."

"I think you should play," said the young woman. "You have such a beautiful voice. You have such a great voice."

Afeyna looked at St. Keith, monks, Rephalah and Muchara. Muchara looked a bit cautious, but the monks and Abbot Keith gave Afeyna hopeful looks. Afeyna looked at the king and boldly said,

"It would be an honor my king."

"Very good," said the queen. "Now we can prepare for a grand banquet"

"Yes," said the king. "Ereigh, give Afeyna the finest robes. She must look great."

"But my, king ... we do this now, said Afeyna"

"Of course. Now I will hear no more," said the king. "You will be standing before chiefs so you must look your best. And be sure to have your song prepared. You will be playing *all* of it before them."

"Yes, my king. Though to be honest, I have never done anything like that."

"You will be fine," said the queen. "Don't worry, you have time. Take whatever time you need to practice."

"Okay."

"Now," said the queen. "Come with me. We have much to talk about."

"Okay," said Afeyna. "Though what it is we are going to talk about?"

"We are just going to spend sometime alone."

Afeyna looked at the queen's face. She seemed welcoming. Muchara stepped up to the two.

"Would it please the queen if I come," Muchara said.

Afeyna saw the stern look on Muchara's face. The atmosphere did seem to change as Muchara and Ereigh looked at each other with a serious expression.

"Why of course," said the queen. "While in fact since you are coming we can invite another."

The queen looked at Rephalah.

"Would you like to come with us?"

Rephalah looked around to see if there is anyone else that the queen may be talking to.

"Yes, I am talking to you," said the queen. "You have the honor of accompanying me."

"With pleasure."

Rephalah quickly walked up the queen. Queen Ereigh looked at Kaleigh.

"You yourself come as well, old lady. If you are able. If not, I understand."

"I am still weary from my travels," said Kaleigh. "I shall do it another time."

"Kaleigh!" said Rephalah.

"It is fine. Let the elder woman rest. Come everyone. Let's spend some time bonding."

"And the men," said Afeyna.

"Leave them," said Ereigh. "I want to get to know you women."

The queen asked one of the guards to fetch them some wine.

"So tell me are you three enjoying your time here at the castle," the queen asked.

"Yes," said Afeyna. "You have been very hospitable."

"I try to be. So tell me Afeyna how were you able to sing like that?"

"It was simply a gift given to me by God. By my king."

"So this 'king' of yours that gifted you is 'Jesus' correct."

"Yes."

"Tell me then. Where does He live. Where is He from."

"He dwells in heaven."

"In heaven," said the queen. "Does that mean you yourselves come from the sky?"

"Well don't come from heaven necesarily."

"But yet you get orders from him? How is that possible."

"The Lord speaks to us from heaven," said Muchara. "We listen to His voice and we follow."

"But have any of you even visited this heaven?"

"No," said Muchara. "But we will go there one day."

"When?"

"On the day we die."

"So this king you serve is a ghost?"

"He is very much alive," said Muchara. "He is the God of all Creation."

The servant came with a tray that had a large jug of wine with pewter cups. The servant poured Rephalah and Muchara's cups and then Ereigh took the bottle from the servant and pour herself and Afeyna a cup of wine. The queen then sent the servant away.

"Afeyna ..." said the queen. "How did you feel about singing to the king."

"I felt a bit nervous but later I felt a bit more confident. To honest I look forward to performing for the king some more."

"And after the banquet, maybe you can stay and be the king's personal musician."

"You really thank so?"

"Why of course."

"That depends that if the Lord would call her to stay," said Muchara. "It is possible that after the banquet we may have to leave."

"But tell me," said the Queen. "But wouldn't her Lord want her to be in the presence of the king? Really, I am sure if her 'Lord' sent her here, then surely it would be beneficial for her to stay wouldn't it."

Muchara gave the queen a cold expression.

"It is not simply for 'Afeyna's benefit, but for the king. If the Lord finds it beneficial for the 'king' then Afeyna will stay."

"Indeed," said Rephalah "It is important I think tha-"

"But Afeyna's talent would be well-served here." The queen said quickly cutting off Rephalah and still looking at Muchara.

"But," said Muchara. "There is a greater purpose."

"And what greater purpose would there be then to serve the queen."

Afeyna saw Ereigh and Rephalah looking at each other intensely. Afeyna and Rephalah froze for a moment. There was a bit of silence in the atmosphere.

"Perhaps," Afeyna said softly. "We could talk about something else. My queen. What do you think about Clehria."

At that moment the queen laughed, and even Muchara had a bit of a laughed.

"I can tell you what I think about *Chlerians*," said Ereigh. "They certain love their venison."

"And why not?" said Afeyna. "They are the best!"

"Indeed they are," said the queen. "Clehrians are quite good and cooking it. Really how do you do? The Rolundans here try to cook it and I find to be a lot tougher than the meat of the Enali region."

"Yes, there is a certain way you have to cook it," said Afeyna. "The venison does taste good with salt and some ale."

"Yes," said Rephalah. "You can also use honey."

"So, Afeyna tell me more about these techniques."

Afeyna explained some of the techniques that she likes to use when she cooks. Rephalah tried to add something but each time she tries, she gets ignored.

"You could," Rephalah would try to say, but each time, the queen asks Afeyna about how to use the technique. The queen never once asked Rephalah. Each time the queen would direct the conversation to Afeyna. Rephalah after being ignored, simply stopped trying to be part of the conversation. At that point Rephalah simply thought about leaving.

Muchara however put her hand on Rephalah's thigh.

"It will soon be over," Muchara whispered to her.

As Rephalah looked at Afeyna receiving a lot of attention from the queen, her heart tightened wth bitterness..

Is this why I left my tribe? To be overshadowed by another?

Rephalah simply sat down and listened to the conversation. She thought about leaving but it would be disrespectful to leave without the queen dissmissing her. Rephalah simply let her mind wander for the rest of the conversation, not paying attention to it.

"Afeyna," said the queen. "You really look at some of the great dresses our tailors have made. I think you will enjoy them."

"Okay."

"Come," said the queen. "I will show you."

"Ok," said Afeyna.

Afeyna looked at Rephlah and Muchara.

33

"Are you all coming."

"Actually," said Rephalah. "I am feeling a little tired. I need to rest a little. I do apologize for offending you."

"It is no problem," said the queen. "You are excused. And you, Muchara. Are you coming? Of course if not. I do understand."

The cold tone by which she said that was noted. Afeyna herself seemed to stiffen a bit when the Muchara and the queen looked at each other.

"To be honest," said Muchara. "I am little bit curious to see these clothes."

There was a bit of silence. Muchara looked at Afeyna.

"What do you say, Afeyna."

"If you want to come, that's fine," said Afeyna. "But I will be fine with the queen. Whatever you want to do.

Muchara sighed.

"I will leave with Rephalah."

"Okay," said Afeyna.

Afeyna and the queen left. The Queen gave Muchara one last glance before leaving. Muchara looked at Rephalah and saw her eyes were a bit watery.

"Are you okay," said Muchara.

"I am fine," said Rephalah. "I am fine."

Muchara gave Rephalah another look.

"Rephalah, I know you."

"Muchara," said Rephalah. "I just don't want to talk about it right now."

"Come on," said Muchara. "Let's go for a walk."

♪ ♪ ♭

"I really do like these!"

Afeyna was in the queen's special room examining the

golden bracelets. One had rubies and emeralds and the other one did not any jewels in it but was still beautiful to look at. Afeyna looked at one particular with instrinsic web-like designs and deer-like designs.

"This one even more beautiful. I love it."

"You really love those types of designs don't you."

"Yes," said Afeyna. "They remind me so much about home."

"But Afeyna," said Alaine, the queen's daughter. "You should look at the ones with the emeralds. This bracelet looks great with your eyes."

"I agree," said the queen.

The queen herself put a necklace with an emerald stone in it.

"Yes, this looks great," said Alaine. "You should definitely wear it to the banquet."

The queen handed Afeyna a mirror, and Afeyna looked. "Wow!"

"You see," said the queen. "You look great."

"Yes!" said Alaine. "You should definitely wear it."

"Okay."

Afeyna looked at the bracelet with the web-like and deer designs.

"Afeyna," said the queen. "The designs on that bracelet looks similar to the one your harp."

"That why I like it."

"If you like it," said the queen. "I suppose you could have it."

"Have it? You mean keep it?"

"What else would I mean? Keep it. It's a gift."

"My queen ... but I ..."

"You would reject a gift from the queen?"

The queen gave Afeyna an irritated glance. Alaine grabbed her arm.

"Afeyna take it," said Alaine. "You wouldn't offend the queen would you."

Afeyna looked the queen's stern expression.

"Okay, my queen."

Afeyna took the bracelet and thanked the queen.

"I think that bracelet suits you well, Afeyna."

"Do you really think so, my queen."

"I know so."

The queen looked at Afeyna's satchel.

"Afeyna," said the queen. "May I have I look at your harp."

"Sure."

Afeyna took the harp out of her satchel and showed it to the queen. The harp has similar web-like designs and antler designs formed the arc of the arc. The harp was made from very fine oak.

"This harp is very beautiful," said the queen. "Where did you get it from."

"Muchara gave it to me."

"Muchara."

The queen took the harp and ran her fingers through the oak.

"Tell me, Afeyna. Who is this Muchara. She seems like an interesting person."

"She comes from Enali. But she has been traveling both Clehria and Rolunda sharing the gospel."

"But I must say for an Enali, she is rather thin. I have seen the Enel people. They are usually tall, strong people. Even their women appear threatening."

"Believe me. Muchara can appear threatening."

"Tell me was she ever a warrior."

"She told she was, but she gave up fighting after a becoming a Christian."

"So she fought for the Enels."

"Yes she does, but she really doesn't talk about it much. Whenever I try to ask her she usually tries to avoid the subject."

"Why? Is is not proud of her warrior past."

"She just said that was who she was in the past. Now she is new person once she gave her life to Christ."

"Interesting."

"You seem very interested in Muchara."

"She just reminds me of an old friend. That's all. Now tell me, Afeyna what is your favorite color?"

"I actually like blue. It's so bright and lovely."

"For a moment, I thought it was green."

"I like green," said Afeyna. "But blue is my favorite."

"Okay then. I will keep that in mind when your robe is designed."

"Great."

♪ ♪ ♭

"I know I should let go, Muchara. I know I should, but it's so hard. It's that whenever I see Afeyna get so much attention, it makes me ask why I even bothered to leave my village. Really the people I have in my travels treat me no different from my husband."

"Believe me I understand," said Muchara. "I myself had to deal with competition. My own husband used to have quite a few women and I had to deal with each of them."

"Why do men do this, Muchara? I was the first love of my husband. I gave him everything and now he treats me as if I am nothing. He himself had his share of women but I stayed the favorite. But now this time …"

"But this time the competition is now more beautiful."
Rephalah chuckled.

"I'm just not as young as I used be. In the past whcn my husband had concubines, I was still the most beautfiul.Now it just isn't the case."

Muchara put her arm around Rephlah.

"I understand the way you feel. Really I do. Time can be very unforgiving. Nonetheless, it is something we must all deal with."

"I know," said Rephalah. "But even to deal with it is hard."

"Well then," said Muchara. "We will deal with it together."

Muchara gave Rephalah a hug.

"Don't be sad, Rephalah. We await a greater world. And in that world all will be restored."

"I know," said Rephalah. "I know."

At that moment Muchara's facial expression changed as she the saw the queen, her daughter and Afeyna walking up to them.

"Afeyna," said Muchara. "Did you get to see your dress."

"I haven't yet but I did get to see some other pretty looking dresses. The queen said she is going to get me fitted for a new dress. I am so excited."

"And don't worry, Muchara," said the queen. "We are going to see if we can get you fitted for something as well."

"You don't have to worry about me."

"But are you are going to be in the presence of the king and his chiefs," said the queen. "I think it will be good for you to dress well."

Muchara said nothing. The queen looked at Rephalah.

"I will have something for you as well of coure."

"Thank you," said Rephalah.

I guess I must be some afterthought now.

"Afeyna," said the queen. "My daughter and I do have something that I have to tend to. But we will talk later okay."

"Okay, my queen." said Afeyna.

The queen left, and after she was gone, Muchara walked up to Afeyna and talked with her.

"How was your time with the queen," said Muchara.

"It was great," said Afeyna. "I enjoyed it very much. She showed me a lot of the beautiful dresses and we talked quite a bit about venison."

"Tell me, Afeyna," said Muchara. "When you talked with the queen. Did anything at all feel off. Did you feel a bit uncomfortable."

"A little. But a royal figure like the queen is going to be a bit intimidating so that is no surprise."

"Afeyna," said Muchara. "Please be careful with that woman. "There is something about her that I do not trust."

"What do you mean, Muchara."

"Just trust me. Don't get too comfortable in her presence."

"Okay, Muchara. Sure."

"I would listen to her," said Rephalah. "I don't really trust her myself."

"You two need to stop worrying. I will be fine. I can take care of myself. After all I have hunted in the past."

"Believe me, Afeyna," said Muchara. "Dealing with the queen is far different to dealing with any wild animals."

"I will be fine, Muchara." Don't worry.

"I hope so, Afeyna. I really do."

♪ ♪ ♭

They sat with Elsiu the high sage in her private room.

"So what do you think of Afeyna."

"Really, I do feel like she is a bit of a threat. My husband has been giving her a lot of attention. I think I do need to find a way to deal with her. Elsiu what do you suppose."

"I think it would be best to wait for a while. Really you have her trust so I think you should take advantage of it."

"Yes, you do make a point. Perhaps it would be best do to wait for the right moment."

"And that woman? What do you think about her?"

"The pale one? Really, I am not sure what to think of her. She does look a bit familiar."

"Indeed," said Elsiu. "The Enel people that I have seen in the past have always been a bit … wider. That one is skinny."

"Yes, and not only that but there is something about her that I cannot put my hands on. You know, not even Afeyna is able to figure out who that woman is. She said she was warrior but she did not say anymore than that."

"Is that so?" said Elsiu. "Hmm … I think it would be good inquire a bit further. Surely that woman must have an agenda."

"I was thinking the same. Her and that fat man."

"Do you think the fat man is using the damsel in order to get the favor of the king."

"It is possible, Elsiu."

"How do you think we should deal with them, my queen?"

"You are the wise one. You tell me, Elsiu."

"I think it would be wise to try to gain their trust. Make them feel comfortable. Learn everything we can about what they are planning. And once we have learned enough, we will strike."

The queen smiled.

"I like that idea, Elsiu. I will do that."

Chapter 4

"In this area the sage would teach me. They taught me from the stone of that pillar."

Afeyna was outside with the princess looking at the stone pillar. From afar the stone appeared large and majestic as it stood atop the hill

"Wow!" said Afeyna. "Can I take a look?"

"Sure," said Alaine.

Afeyna ran up the hill to see the pillar and it was quite large being more than five times Afeyna's size. And all over the pillar was written inscriptions detailing the epic sagas. There were even pictures that gave a bit of detail on the sagas. Afeyna rubbed her hand across the stone.

"Wow!" said Afeyna. "To have the epic sagas right here in stone. What a feeling. I feel close to McFurru already."

"Can you read it?"

"No. Sadly I never learned to read. But I can look at some of these inscriptions and get a bit of an idea of what is going on. Like that picture. It looks be an image of McFurru fighting Elnia in order to get the white horse."

"Yes, and that right is the golden spear forged by Balnur by the fires of the sun."

"Wow," said Afeyna. "This is great. Alaine, can you read it to me. Some of it at least."

"Sure. '*And McFurru looked at the dragon with fire burning in his eyes. A fire that was so bright and so strong that the fires of the dragon seemed like little embers in comparison. McFurru standing strong and with his spear clenched was ready to release his manly grip and his spear would fly from his and hand and toward the dragon.*'

"'*The dragon breathed fire at the spear, but that only made the spear shine brighter as it when throught the belly of the dragon, tearing its heart and painting the golden spear red with the blood of the dragon.*'"

"Alaine even as you speak every word to me I am able to picture the scene in my head. You are a great reader. I really felt like I was in the story."

"Believe me. When I was young I used to love reading these stories. I actually used to spend many days reading the stories on this tablet. I was actually very obsessed with this stone. Every day I would spend hours here. My mother was actually starting to worry bit because every chance I had, I would run."

"It must have been great to hear all of those different stories told."

"It was. It always felt like I was right there with the heroes whenever I was around this tablet."

Afeyna rubbed the tablet again.

"Wow."

Afeyna continued to look at the stone.

"Afeyna," said Alaine. "Do the monks have their own stories written in stone?"

"Actually," said Afeyna. "We write our stories down on paper. We actually have manuscripts for our stories."

"Really? Could I take a look?"

"Sure I don't have them myself. I would have to ask St. Keith, but I am sure he would be willing to show you."

"I would love that."

"But I doubt that you would be able to read them though. They are not written in the Illish language."

"Ah, so its written in a foreign language?"

"What is this language called?"

"I think is is called *Latin*. It is the language spoken on the Continent."

"Is that so? What does it sound like. I have always been curious about life is beyond the sea."

"It is a pretty language. Though to be honest I don't know much of it myself."

"Well whenever you get the chance will you show me?"

"Of course. I might be able to show you later on today."

"That would be great."

There was silence for a moment.

"Afeyna," said Alaine. "Were you always able to sing so well."

"Well, my village would say I would. In fact in Chlehria I use to sing for my father almost every night. He would love hearing me sing about the great McFurru."

"Yes, and it seems like *my own* father would like to keep you around for a bit. He probably might want you to stay so you could sing for more many more nights to come."

"If the Lord would have me do that, then it is okay with. I am here to glorify Him."

"You speak quite fondly of your lord."

"That is because He is wonderful and He has done a lot for me. He has comforted me when I was downcast and He has be put a new song in my heart," Afeyna begun to sing, "*He has lifted me from the dust and has allowed me stand before kings.*"

Afeyna chuckled for a moment.

"I am sorry. I couldn't help myself for a moment. I just had to sing. Often when I talk about the Lord my heart just has to sing."

Alaine laughed for a moment.

"I understand. I would like to meet your Lord one day. You must introduce me to him some day."

"I can introduce you to him now if you would like."

Alaine looked at Afeyna with wide eyes.

"But how would you do that? Are you able to summon him?"

"Yes. In fact all who calls on the name of the Lord will be saved."

"Saved? From what?"

"From perishing in your sins When our first father Adam sinned against God it caused us to fall into sin. Man was unable to reconcile himself to God so God himself had to come down reconcile us to Him. He became a man and died for us."

"I understand a little. There are still question I have like how did reconcile man to himself by dying and how did man 'sin'. This all seems complicated."

"Don't worry. The Lord the will reveal Himself to you if you ask. 'Seek and you will find.'"

"Okay then. I don't understand much but am I little bit intrigued."

♪ ♪ ♭

"I must say say this stew is very good."

One of the queen's servants tried the monks' stew.

"At the monastery that all we cook," said Mark, one of the monks. "We have become masters of the craft."

"Indeed. You cook the meet very tender."

The monks, Muchara, and Rephalah were with the servants in the hot kitchen cooking.

"Mark here is one of the best cooks we have," said Muchara. "If you can think of it, he can cook it."

"To be fair," said Mark. "It was Rephalah, she helped me a lot as well."

"That soup is actually a favorite of my husband's," said Rephalah.

"You should definitely cook for the banquet. Your help would be most appreciated."

"Would there even be enough food for the chiefs."

"We always have plenty of cows so it would be no problem. Really though its the venison. We are getting a few sent here. But I am not sure it will be enough."

"No worries," said Malcolm another monk. "I am sure we will find some way to stretch it. We ourselves don't have that many cattle at the monastery so we had to find a way to make it last."

"Well if you would all stay just to help for the banquet, your help would be most appreciated."

The servant at that point gave a grave expression.

"My queen," said the servant.

Everyone in the kitchen quickly went back to work.

"Why do I hear little talking and no working . And why are you all here?"

"My queen," said the servant. "We were a little short-staffed and they decided to help."

When the queen looked at the monks, they stiffened and became timid and quite. But Muchara went forward and said,

"It is not their fault. We decided to help. They told we did not have to but they offered."

The atmosphere quickly began tense as Muchara and the queen looked at each other.

"If you want to to help you should ask. Normally we don't like to have guest here," said the queen.

"I thought the queen would be okay with getting a little help in the kitchen," said Muchara.

"We are just fine without outside help. If we need your help I will ask for it."

Everyone in the kitchen stiffened a bit as the atmosphere seem to get a bit colder. The queen looked at the bowl of soup.

"That smells good."

"Would you like to try," said Muchara. "*I* cooked it myself."

The queen took a spoon and tasted the soup.

"Not bad for an outsider."

Muchara smirked at the queen.

"Not bad for an *outsider,*wouldn't you say."

"If you want to stay here and help you can for *today*. But afterwords I do not want to see you in *my* kitchen."

The queen looked at the leader of the cooks.

"Borus. You can allow them to stay help for today, but afterwards I do not want to see them here. Understood?"

"Yes, my queen. Understood. Thank you."

The queen left the room. Everyone wanted to make sure that she was away from the kitchen before saying anything.

"Muchara," said Borus the servant. "You did not need to talk to the queen like that."

Muchara still had a stern expression.

"Borus, I do apologize for getting you in trouble. It's just that as a proud warrior, I couldn't just let her talk down to me."

"But she is the queen. Respect is due."

"I scarcely give *any* respect to someone like that."

The servants did seem a bit uncomfortable. Muchara sighed.

"I apologize," Muchara said.

"You should be careful what you say. You never know who is listening."

"I'm a warrior. I don't live in fear," said Muchara.

The cooks looked at Muchara in silence.

"I'm sorry," said Muchara. "I will trouble you know more."

Muchara was about to leave but one of the cooks stopped her.

"Muchara, you don't have to leave. We do enjoy having you."

"You have all been good to me. But I don't want to cause you any further trouble."

Muchara left and Rephalah followed after her.

The servants to with the monks about Muchara.

"I must say, the Enel people are certain feisty group."

"Yes, they are," said Mark. "But still … even for an Enel the treatment of the queen is a bit surprising."

♪ ♪ ♭

"Muchara, what was that all about? Are you okay," said Rephalah.

"Yes, I am," Muchara said with a sigh. "I am not sure what got to me, Rephalah. Really that queen just gets on my nerves sometimes."

"Mine too," said Rephalah. "I respect her rule … but still. Whenever I look at her face I do cringe at times."

"I am really that ugly that you would do that?"

Rephalah quickly jumped when she heard the queen ask that question.

"Queen Ereigh."

As Rephalah stiffened a bit, she noticed the queen give her smirk. Clearly she enjoys watching people cower in her presence.

"Queen," said Muchara. "I didn't see you. Where were standing off somewhere?"

"You could say that I was."

"To what honor do we owe the pleasure of your presence," said Rephalah.

"Muchara!" said the queen. "I don't like the way you spoke you to spoke to me in front of my servants."

Rephalah sighed as the queen ignored her fixing her attention on Muchara.

"What do you mean," said Muchara. "I was being as polite as I could be."

"If *that* was your most polite then I suppose it is to be expected. Really, I guess, I shouldn't expect that much more from an Enel."

"For an Enel chief the way I talked would've been considered polite."

The queen approached Muchara a little bit so they could look at each other a little more closely. Rephalah marveled that Muchara did not even budge.

Really Muchara you are strong woman.

"Listen to me, Enel. I want you to know that you are *not* in Enali said the queen. And here we treat our royalty with a bit more respect. The way you treated me I could kill you but since you are just a simple Enel barbarian, I will be merciful enough to let you off with a warning.

"Don't ever treat me like *that* in front of anyone they way ever again. In fact don't treat me like that in front of anyone again period. Because if you do, we may just have more problems. Do you understand."

Rephalah felt the cold silence but Muchara still stood firm. In fact Muchara simply gave a very firm answer.

"Perfectly."

"Enel," the queen continued. "I can be gracious person.

But believe me you do *not* want to see me when I am not so gracious."

Muchara simply smirked at little. The queen smirked also.

"Keep on smiling. You might eventually find that smirk removed from your face."

With that, the queen walked off. Muchara and Rephalah were now alone. Rephalah whispered,

"Muchara you might have to be bit careful."

"Careful of what?" said Muchara. "I am a born warrior. I fear noone. If anything she is the one who should be careful."

♪ ♪ ♭

While the queen was walking through the corridor, she thought about Muchara's face.

Who does that woman think she is? She has some nerve talking to me like that.

As the queen thought more about Muchara's face a thought came to her.

I wonder ... could it be her? *Only* she *would have the nerve to stand up to me like that.*

The queen thought some more.

"So *Muchara.* Is it really *you?* How nice of you to return. I will have to find a way to welcome you."

♪ ♪ ♭

Afeyna and Alaine walked the hallway talking more about the Gospel. While talking they ran into Muchara and Rephalah. Afeyna noticed that Muchara seemed a little bit troubled.

"Hi, Muchara. Are you feeling okay?"

"I feel fine," said Muchara. "I see you two have been getting along well."

"We have," said Afeyna. "Me and Alaine have been talking the tales of old and also about the Gospel."

Muchara smiled.

"I am glad to hear that."

Muchara looked at Alaine.

"What do you think about the gospel," said Muchara.

"It's interesting. There are still some things I don't understand, but I am intrigued."

"I was going to take her see St. Keith's Latin translation of the Gospels."

"Ah, that is great! Though St. Keith is a little busy."

"Busy! What is he is doing?"

"Apparently he is helping to make leather pouch."

Afeyna chucked a bit.

"St. Keith always have to do something to stay busy.!"

Muchara chuckled.

"You know Abbot Keith. He is a hard worker."

"It seems that a lot of you have been trying to help around the castle," said Alaine. "I heard you were helping to prepare a meal in the castle."

"We like hospitality," said Muchara. "But we prefer to do the serving rather than do the serving. That was how our Lord was like when he walked the earth. He served many people."

"Your Lord serves others?"

"Why of course," said Muchara. "He died for humanity as a man. He is the best servant of all."

"I do your Lord to be interesting. I am learning more about him," said Alaine.

"And I hope you continue to learn more about Him. Come, If you want to see a manuscript I can show you."

"I would like that," said Alaine.

The group followed Muchara but Rephalah stayed behind.

"Are you not coming?" Afeyna said to her.

"I am staying behind," said Rephalah. "I am feeling a little tired."

"You don't want to look at the manuscript?"

"I've seen the manuscript multiple times already," said Rephalah. "It is just a colorful sheet of paper."

"Get some rest Rephalah," said Muchara. "Be ready for dinner."

Rephalah walked off. When Rephalah walked off Afeyna looked at Muchara.

"The nerve of her!" said Afeyna. "To call the Scriptures just 'a colorful piece of paper.'"

"She didn't mean it, Afeyna," said Muchara. "She is tired."

"Yes I am sure she is just *tired*. Really, I understand that she has a lot on her mind, but really she does need to get over herself."

"Come see the manuscripts," said Muchara. "Let's go."

Alaine saw Afeyna sigh and then smile. She saw Afeyna quickly calm down

"Fine, let's go."

They went to to look at the manuscripts.

♪ ♪ ♭

"So what do you think of that," said the Abbot.

The servant of the king looked at the pouch.

"I must say, I am very impressed with the quality of this."

St. Keith chuckled.

"I have been making pouches like these for a very long time. In fact a man who came from the Continent showed me."

"Amazing."

The king entered the room.

"So how are things," he said.

"They are fine my king," said the servant. "Abbot was just helping us out."

"Is that so?"

The king looked at the pouch that St. Keith had made.

"This looks good."

"That was designed by the abbot my king," said the servant.

The king looked at Abbot Keith.

"I must say I am impressed. The style looks a little bit different."

"He said he learned from someone who came from the continent."

The king gave a shocked expression.

"Is that so?" said the king.

The king examined the pouch a little bit more.

"Tell me what was the name of this man."

"His name is St. Brendan he was very great man."

"Very interesting. I have heard a long time ago about a stranger that landed on this island. I heard he traveled through much of Clehria."

"And part of Rolunda also."

"And you know this man?"

"Of course."

"You must tell me about him over dinner."

"Why course. He is the one who told us about Jesus."

The king's tone then changed.

"Tell me is still alive?"

"That is not known," said a monk. "After staying for a few years he left the island, and he was never heard from again. St. Keith now takes on the responsibility of sharing the gospel."

"I have to wander if this 'Brendan' was as interesting as you."

"He was *very* interesting. In fact I am rather boring compared to him."

"Then perhaps it is better that I *don't* meet him," said the king. "*You* yourself are interesting enough."

Abbot Keith and servant laughed. As they were talking, Elsiu entered the room. He glared at St. Keith for a moment and then looked away.

"My king," said Elsiu.

"Dinner is ready."

"Thank you, Elsiu."

Elsiu walked away.

"Come," said the king let us enjoy.

♪ ♪ ♭

"So what do you think?"

"It is so beautiful," said Alaine.

Muchara showed them a page of the Scripture. It was a part of the Latin Bible translated by the monks. Afeyna always enjoyed looking at the Bible each time St. Keith took it out. He placed the Book in front of Afeyna. The very letter of the first page was very well colored. The letter was enclosed in a square with colorful web-like designs and the each letter was curvy dark and pointy.

It was clear that a lot of time went into making this book. Afeyna stroked the pages.

"What does it say," said Alaine. "I can't really read it."

Muchara began reading it for her. It was John 1:1 of the Latin Vulgate.

"In principio erat verbum. Verbum cum Deo erat et Verbum Deus erat. In the beginning was the Word. The Word was with God and the Word was God."

"It is talking about Jesus isn't it?"

"Yes, it is," said Muchara. "He both is God and with God."

"So there are two gods."

"No only one."

Alaine seemed a bit confused. Muchara chuckled a bit.

"I know. I it is great mystery. But the way Abbot Keith used to explain it to me was like this: It is like a clover. You have three leaves but there is one stem. Sure you have three people, but they are one God."

"Three?"

"That is a subject for another time. But do you understand a little better."

"A little."

"You will. I see God revealing more and more Himself to you each day."

Alaine turned a page of the manuscript. She saw picture of a man being baptized in water and a dove hovering over him.

"Is that your Lord," said Alaine.

"Yes, it is," said Muchara.

"What is he doing being dipped in water?"

"He is being baptized."

"Baptized?" said Alaine.

"Yes, in order to receive the power of God and show that you are truly His own you get baptized."

"And that is when you are dipped in water."

"Yes. I know it is a bit complex, but you will undestand it little by little."

There was a knock on the door.

"Enter," said Muchara.

It was the queen.

"Mother," said Alaine.

The queen saw Muchara holding a manuscript in her hand.

"Alaine, were you in the middle of something," the queen said.

"Mother, Muchara was showing me a manuscript. It is about her Lord."

The queen gave Muchara a glaring looked. Muchara returned the glare. Alaine looking at the two, quickly felt tense.

"Mother," said Alaine."Is there something you need?"

"I was just coming to let you know that dinner is almost ready. You all should dress nicely. You all will be eating before the king"

"Yes, mother. Alaine, come with me," said the Queen.

"Yes ma'am."

Alaine left the room with the queen. Afeyna was alone with Muchara. Afeyna saw that Muchara was a bit stiff herself.

"Are you okay," said Afeyna.

"I am fine," said Muchara.

"It seems to be the opposite."

"No, really I am."

Muchara sighed.

"Afeyna," said Muchara.

"Please careful with that woman, Afeyna. There is just something about her."

"But Muchara, she does not seem that bad. She is a gracious person."

"Afeyna," said Muchara. "You can call an eagle 'gracious,' but it is still deadly. It still has talons."

Afeyna put her hand on Afeyna.

"Be wise Afeyna."

♪ ♪ ♭

The queen walked alongside Alaine to the banqueting hall. Alaine was sharing with the queen all that she learned about the Lord.

"So this 'Lord' of theirs died to save others. That seems a bit baffling."

"But I do find it to be a bit intriguing."

"And the monks wrote that manuscript that you were just looking at."

"Yes. They are very skilled. I am intrigued."

"Well don't get too 'intrigued,' Alaine. Really those monks do seem a bit strange."

"How so …"

"I just find their god to be a little bit peculiar."

"I will admit that He is a bit interesting. But you know we have many gods. And a lot of them have their peculiarities."

"Yes, that is true," said the queen. "But still … dying for humanity."

"The forest spirit Uch'lein died for his lover."

"Yes, but that is woman he loves. This 'Lord' that the monks speak of died for the whole of humanity … People he does not know."

"But in a way when a person dies for a stranger that can be considered loving."

"You would say loving. I would say a bit foolish."

Alaine said nothing more.

"Come, Alaine, cheer up," said the queen. "We are just making conversation. Now come let us continue our conversation at dinner. The king awaits us."

"Yes, Mother"

♪ ♪ ♭

"So God became man to save man," said the king. "That is interesting."

"Yes, and this is the wonderful news of the gospel."

Everyone was seating at the table for the feast. It was as a long table. The king sat at the head of the table and Afeyna and the Queen each sat on one side of the king.

"Really, Abbot," said the Queen. "How could your god even die for people he did not know. I have heard of a god dying for a lover. But one dying for people. Tell me, abbot why would he do that?"

"What makes you think he didn't know the humans he died for?"

"Are you saying he knew *every* single human?"

"Off course. In fact he knew every single human before they were born."

"Ah, so your god is an oracle. He knows the future."

"Yes, in fact, I would I say he knows the past present *and* the future."

"Interesting. So he is a god of time."

"Indeed," said the Abbot. "He is a God time, nature, life, love, power, and wisdom. He is a God of *all*."

"But how can that be?" said Ereigh? "No god can every be *that* powerful."

"Mine is."

"Abbot!" said the king. "That is a strong statement. You are saying she is even more powerful *than* Ilruna, the mother goddess."

"Indeed," said St. Keith. "And this God would like for you to know Who He is."

"Hmmm," said the king. "To have a God like that, I would be the most powerful king in Illunra. Noone would be able to oppose me."

"Actually," said St. Keith. "This God would like for *you* to serve *Him* and be part of His kingdom."

The queen rose up.

"Do you see what this monk is saying," said the queen. "He wants you to *surrender*."

"Why of course," said the Abbot. "To the God of *all* creation."

"Creation? So now you are saying He created everything?"

"Yes, my queen. The Lord is already revealing more of Himself to you," Abbot Keith said with a laugh.

The queen sighed.

"Really monk you do love to try the royal family," said the Queen.

"What do you mean," said St. Keith. "I simply want to share the riches of the truth of the gospel and of the Lord Jesus Christ."

"Tell me, abbot," said the queen with a cold look. "When you say the king should the surrender to your god are you saying that he should surrender to *you*."

"Who am *I*," said St. Keith. "That the king would surrender to *me*. I am pointing to Someone far *greater* … One whose shoes am not even worthy to untie."

"Is that so," said the queen. "Well if he is so great, how about he show himself. How about he do something. And if he does I will be willing to surrender," said Ereigh. "Come on, i am waiting."

At that point there was a very loud thunder. It was so loud and so clear that it made the queen herself jump. Muchara looked at the queen.

"Did that scare you," said Muchara with a smile.

The queen looking at the monks and the sages that were at the table blushed a little.

58

"I was only a little surprised."

Alaine who sat next to the queen looked out the window and the evening was clear. There was no rain.

"Amazing," said Alaine. "It's not raining."

"Do not flatter them," said the queen as she sat down.

"Where's your boldness," said Muchara. "Did the Lord scare you with a bit of thunder."

"You best watch your tongue, Enel," said the queen, "I know you pride yourself a warrior, but so do I."

"But i said," Muchara, "am a warrior the powerful God on her side."

"I have many gods," said Ereigh. "What's one God to me."

"Believe me. My one God is more than enough"

There was once again a tense atmosphere when the two looked at each other. Everyone was silent. Even Abbot Keith kept silent for a moment. The tense atmosphere was quickly softened by the smell of food.

"Now," said the king. "I believe that is enough talk about gods for one evening. Let us simply enjoy ourselves."

"Yes, milord," said the Queen.

Muchara simply nodded.

"Yes, king."

The maidservants gave everyone at the table their meal. The king was about to eat but Abbot Keith stopped him.

"Before we eat we should always say grace."

"Grace?" the king said with a confused look.

"We give thanks to the Lord for allowing us to enjoy this food."

"What do you mean we should thank your god," said Ereigh. "Your god did not cook this meet nor did he prepare it."

"But," said Abbot Keith. "He did created the creatures that

we eat and He created the herbs that your servants and these lovely damsels would prepare."

"Really," the queen. "I am not believing this."

"Enough," said the king. "I thought we agreed that this conversation would cease for the moment."

"My apologies," said the abbot. "You are right. But I thought it be fitting to give thanks. Don't you think my king."

Everyone looked at the king. The king sighed.

"Very well."

"Now everyone," said Abbot Keith. "Let us bow our heads in reverence."

The people that were with Abbot Keith bowed their heads but the others looked reluctant. They still bowed.

"Oh, Lord, we thank you for this food and we also thank you for the glorious opportunity of sharing your love with those at this table. Please let your favor be upon the king and bless this food amen."

Everyone then started eating. They enjoyed their food and they mingled and talked among each other. Abbot Keith answered questions that the king had, and the monks and sages had a bit of a debate as.

The queen saw the king talking to Afeyna. Afeyna glanced at the queen and seemed a bit nervous. The king asked Afeyna how she felt about the upcoming banquet.

"A little nervous," she said. "When I perform there will be chiefs sitting at this table."

"You will be fine," said the queen. "I will make sure you good for the banquet."

"Thank you, my queen."

After the banquet the king asked to be alone with Afeyna. The queen saw king take Afeyna away. The queen looked and simply walked away. Muchara seeing this simply uttered a prayer.

"Oh, Lord please be with Afeyna."

♪ ♪ ♭

Elsiu walked with queen through the corridor. It was about nighttime.

"So, my queen," said Elsiu. "How are you going to deal with Afeyna?"

"Don't worry, Elsiu. I will deal with her. The banquet is coming up soon so there will be plenty of time to deal with her."

Chapter 5

Afeyna was in the quiet courtyard with the king enjoying the smell of roses on that starry night.

"Afeyna how do you feel about being here," said the king.

"It is great," said Afeyna. "I've been treated very well here, and the queen has been very gracious."

"I am glad you enjoy yourself, Afeyna. Tell me, Afeyna after the banquet, how you like to stay here."

"To stay? My king … I am not sure."

"Afeyna, you could be my musician here and enjoy many great privileges."

"I would have to think about it."

"What is there to think about?" said the king.

"I would have to ask God what He thinks. Please," said Afeyna. "May I please have time to think about it."

"That is fine," said the king.

♪ ♪ ♭

Rephalah was in her room straightening up and there was a knock at the door.

"Come in," she said.

Muchara entered.

"How are you doing doing," said Muchara, "Are you feeling okay."

"I am feeling, fine," said Rephalah. "How you are you."

Rephalah saw the grave look on the Muchara's face.

"Are you okay," said Rephalah. "You seem troubled."

"Rephalah," said Muchara. "I have been burdened for Afeyna all night. I have had some difficulties sleeping. I have spent most of the night praying."

"Is it because of the queen," said Rephalah.

"Yes," said Muchara. "I don't trust her. And also I thought about the banquet. I have a bad feeling about."

"Should we tell Afeyna," said Rephalah.

"The sooner she knows the better."

♪ ♪ ♭

Afeyna was in the courtyard playing her harp in the warm sun. She was playing for hours praising the Lord and reciting hyms. Muchara came up to her.

"Afeyna," said Muchara.

"Hi, Muchara. Are you doing okay?"

"I am doing fine and yourself?"

"Great! Are you feeling okay? You like you have something on your mind."

"We need to talk," said Muchara. "But quietly."

"Okay."

Muchara sat next to Afeyna.

"Afeyna," said Muchara softly. "What happened between you and the king last night?"

"Nothing really," said Afeyna. "We just having a conversation."

"So you did not do *anything?*"

"No," said Afeyna. "We just had conversation and that was all."

"About what?"

"Muchara, you really are curious, aren't you?"

"I just worry about you, Afeyna. I just don't want you to get into a dangerous situation."

"I am fine," said Afeyna. "I can take care of myself. And besides the queen herself is really gracious."

"I am going to tell you this, Afeyna. The queen herself is a fox. She may try to be your friend but in the end she will attempt to end you."

"And how do you know that, Muchara? You act as if you know her."

Muchara was silent.

"Afeyna, I worry for you."

"How so? The queen has been very good to me. She has treated me well."

"Afeyna … surely you must know that there is something about her. You see how she gave you were with the king."

Afeyna shrugged her shoulders.

"That is her husband. So I understand that she might feel a little suspicious."

"Afeyna … be careful."

"Everything will be fine."

"I hope so. I will keep you in prayer."

"I don't think that will even be necessary. But i do appreciate the concern."

Afeyna got up.

"I do have get ready for the banquet. The queen is having me try out some new ornaments for the dress."

Afeyna was about to walk off but Muchara asked Afeyna another question.

"Just one more thing, Afeyna. Did the queen at all ask you anything about me."

"Yes, and I told her you are a good friend and that we have many travels together. Why?"

"It is nothing."

"No, I would like to know why you asked."

"I was just wondering that's all."

♪ ♪ ♭

"I am not surprised," said Rephalah. "Afeyna can be stubborn."

"I hope Afeyna is not letting all that attention get to her," said Muchara. "She has been receiving a lot."

"Indeed. She has been receiving a lot of admiration from the king and from the sages."

"Rephalah," said Muchara. "We must keep Afeyna in prayer."

Rephalah nodded.

"She will need all that she can get."

♪ ♪ ♭

"The dress looks so much better."

Afeyna was in the chamber room with the queen examining the dress with its gold trimming and web-like designs.

"I would asked the tailor to touch it up a little bit. I want you to look nice for the banquet."

Afeyna froze for moment.

The banquet.

"Is everything okay, Afeyna?" said the queen.

"Yeah, everything is fine. I was just thinking about something."

"About what? Is seems rather serious that for it to cause you freeze."

Afeyna looked at the queen's concerned looked. Or least

she seems concerned. There was in a feeling in the heart that was difficult to shake.

The banquet.

"It's nothing my queen."

"Are you sure. Is it something that Muchara said?"

"Well …"

Afeyna could not say anything else.

"I thought as much. She told you I was dangerous didn't you?"

"How did you …"

"Afeyna, when a person sees another with the queen it is natural for them to feel a little jealous."

"Do you really think so?"

"I know so. Not that I blame her. That reaction is natural. She and her friend seem to have a dislike for me … or for you."

"I mean …"

"You know it's true, Afeyna. You see how Muchara looks at me, and also the way her friend looks at you. She seems bitter."

Afeyna was silent.

"But they are my friends."

"You may think they are friends, but often when they see someone else doing better they often are jealous. Afeyna, I been gracious to them. I allowed to wear nice clothes and eat at the king's table. And yet they still do not show gratitude. They may say it with their lips but their faces say it all."

"Yeah … you do have a point."

The queen saw Afeyna seemed a little downcast.

"Don't let what I say get you down. You are a very gifted person, Afeyna, and there are those that would be jealous of that. Understand that."

"I am understand my queen."

"Come now cheer up. Look, I want you to see what I got for you."

The queen showed Afeyna a golden harp. Afeyna gasped.

"My queen!"

"Since you are you going to be preforming before the king you should have a new harp."

"I love it!" said Afeyna

"Now that you have that harp you have no need for that old wooden one."

"But that harp is precious to me. It to me as a gift."

"From Muchara?"

"Yes."

"I understand but the gold one would look great for the banquet."

"Thank you."

♪ ♪ ♭

"And Lord please protect Afeyna and keep her. Amen"

As she prayed Rephalah had a difficult time concentrating. She thought about Afeyna. She walked to her window and looked outside at the cloudy sky. She sighed.

"Why does Afeyna get all of the attention. And often I am getting ignored."

Rephalah thought about her travels with the group, and how Afeynae each time got attention from others: The villagers, the monks, the servants of th castle, the queen and the king. Rephalah sighed.

"Was it even a good idea to leave?"

Rephalah though a lot on her past.

If only I could be young again.

Kaleigh, her maidservant entered the room

"Have you finished praying," said Kaleigh.

"I have. I am just thinking."

"You always seem to have a lot on your mind."

"I know. Kaleigh, what have you thought about our travels so far?"

"I have enjoyed them. The monks have treated me very well and I have enjoyed listening to Afeyna."

"Afeyna ... everyone seems to love her."

Kaleigh put her hand on Rephalah's.

"Getting older is difficult isn't. You would receive a lot of attention from other in your youth and as you get older you slowly see that attention go away."

"So you understand how I feel?"

"Understand? I lived it. Rephalah, you know I was in a similar situation when *you* were young. You know I was actually jealousy of you a several years ago."

Rephalah gave a shocked expression.

"Really?"

"I used to watch how you would receive a lot of attention. I always hated it."

"I didn't know that you used to feel that way."

"To be honest even in my youth, I wasn't all that attractive so even then I had to deal with feeling inferior to others. I remember when I saw you growing up and getting attention from men. In some ways I often tried to live through you."

Rephalah chuckled a bit.

"I guess what Muchara says is true. The past does repeat itself. You used to feel jealously towards me and now I feel jealously towards Afeyna."

"Time is hard to deal with at times," said Kaleigh. "It not only affects you physically but mentally. Believe me, I know."

Rephalah put her hand Kaleigh's.

"Sometimes I long so much to have those days back. I think

to myself if I could be young again. If only i could have my beauty back. Everytime i see Afeyna I am reminded of that fact."

"You know if Muchara were here she would say, you should look towards the future. The past is the past. Doesn't Muchara often talk about a world to come? How in that world, wounds will be healed and the things of this world will be forgotten."

"Yes," said Rephalah. "I think about that."

"When I think of that. In many ways that was what attracted me to the gospel," said Kaleigh. "This new world in which there will be everlasting joy, and peace. The though of it feels me with joy."

"Yes, me too," said Rephalah with a smile.

She gave Kaleigh a hug.

"Thank you, Kaleigh. You know how to make me feel better."

"I care for you Rephalah. I too felt bitter. As you got older and I saw how the chief's new wife interfered in your life, I felt for you. There were times I got jealous, but as you got older, that was when I finally started to see a little bit of myself in you."

Rephalah laughed.

"Kaleigh you are cheering me up! Don't bring me down now."

Kaleigh and Rephalah laughed and hugged each other.

"Kaleigh," said Rephalah. "In many ways you are more a friend to me than a servant. Whenever I feel down you always know how to cheer me up."

"I have known you for a long time, Rephalah. Ever since you were a baby. So of course I know you well."

Rephalah kissed Kaleigh on the forehead.

"And I as I have gotten older I have come to know you well."

The two smiled at each other and continued to look out the window and continued to enjoy the view together.

♪ ♪ ♭

Afeyna went back to her room, and looked at her harp. She had on her latern and the golden harp gleamed brightly in the light. Afeyna's heart beat with excited.

I am so excited. In just a few days, I will get to preform at the banquet.

Afeyna looked at the harp and played on the strings. It played far better then the wooden harp that Muchara gave her.

"What an honor to receive such a harp."

There was a knock on the door.

"Come in," said Afeyan.

It was Muchara.

"Oh … hi Muchara," said Afeyna.

"You don't look … very happy to see me."

"I am happy. Really I am."

Muchara looked at the harp.

"The queen gave you that harp didn't she."

"Yes, it was very kind of her. I can really see God bestowing me His favor."

"Afeyna …" said Muchara. "I feel that you are being put in a dangerous situation."

"Dangerous? What do you mean?"

"As I told you before. The queen is a fox. She knows how to destroy others to get what she wants."

"Muchara, what are you talking about?"

"Afeyna open your eyes. Can you not see she is playing

you? The harp, dress. She is trying to win you over so she can destroy you."

"Why are you so hard on the queen," said Afeyna. "She has been nothing but gracious to you!"

"You don't know that woman like-"

"Like what! Like you. How do you claim to know so much about her? You are just a woman who came from a desert. You have never even seen her before."

"Oh, but I have seen her."

"But how?"

"How do you think I ended up in the wildereness in the first place?"

"What are you saying?"

"I know that woman. We were rivals at one time."

"What?"

"Afeyna. Tha war that happened many years ago. I was the one that led it. A long time ago, I fought against the queen. The civil war that happened fifteen years ago. I was a leader in that war. I fought against the queen but I lost. She would've killed me but I escaped. I ran to the wilderness so that she would not find me."

Afeyna looked shocked for a moment. But then she laughed.

"What is so funny," said Muchara.

"You had me for a moment, Muchara."

"Whatt do you mean? I was being serious."

"Yes, but if you really fought in that war, how it is the queen did not recognize you?"

"I ... was a much heftier person then."

"Why did you wait until *now* to tell me."

"Because I was hoping it would not be necesary to tell you. I hoping this would just be a momentary visit and then we leave."

"That also makes me ask. If this has been true whole time, then why did you hide this from me. All this time we shared together and traveled you kept this from me. Why?"

"Afeyna, I did it because I believed it for the better that *noone* knew. Tell would it be good for a known enemy of the queen to be wandering throughout Illunra."

"But Muchara. We are friends. Don't you trust me to keep your secret."

"It was a past that I wanted noone to know about. I wanted to have a new beginning."

"And you worried if I knew then I would only see the 'old' Muchara and not the new one."

Muchara did not respond.

"Muchara, the scripture says when one is in Christ, she is a new creature. Why would you worry that?"

"Perhaps it was wrong, Afeyna. But I did what knew best."

"To keep secrets? What else are you hiding?"

"Afeyna, let us focus on the matter at hand. Listen. You must be careful with the queen. She does not have your best interest at heart."

"But she spent so much time helping me prepare for the Banquet of Chiefs."

"And believe me she is preparing you for something."

Afeyna took her harp and was about to walk out.

"Afeyna, where are you going."

"I am going to get some fresh air."

"Afeyna, please be careful. I am sorry for not sharing with you my past but I really do care for you."

"Tell me, Muchara, I would like to know. Did you do something to make the queen angry? She is gracious. Maybe *you* did something to anger *her!*"

"Absolutely not! Afeyna listen to me. That woman took from me someone that I cared about. I to avenge him."

"But what did *he* do."

Muchara could not answer.

"Perhaps maybe its just *you* who should watch the queen." Afeyna walked out.

♪ ♪ ♭

Rephalah was in her room thinking. There was a knock on the door.

"Come in."

Muchara came in and before she said anything, Rephalah said,

"Let me guess. It is about Afeyna isn't it?"

Muchara chuckled.

"I do talk about her a lot."

"And when you are not talking about her, you are talking about the queen."

"I am sorry, Rephalah. It's just that I do wonder if I should have came here. Ever since coming here, I had a bad feeling. And now I understand why."

"I too, began to feel the same. At first, I was excited, but admitedly after seeing Afeyna get so much attention and getting to know the queen, I did begin to feel a bit uncomfortable here."

"Really, Rephalah, I do believe it will be important to pray."

Rephalah nodded.

"You are right. Let us pray together."

♪ ♪ ♭

"Alaine, are you excited about the banquet."

"Yes, I am! I can't wait I wonder what Afeyna is going to play."

"I myself am wondering. Do you have your own wardrobe ready. I know have been so focused on Afeyna that I have neglected you."

"I understand. This banquet is a big event. I understand your worry. You want Afeyna to preform well before the chiefs and the kings."

"Yes, I do."

"Mother, the message that Afeyna has been teaching. It is rather interesting isn't it."

The queen nodded.

"Yes it is intriguing. It is not something that I would believe but it interesting nonethless."

"Yes this idea of a dying God is very interesting."

"Alaine, I understand Muchara's religion is intriguing,but really I would not think to much about it. To be honest it always seemed rathers strange."

"I know. That is why I do find it to be a bit interesting."

"Alaine, I would be careful with them."

"Why would you say that?"

"It is just a feeling I have. You know from the way they talk, it seems like they believe that their god is the only true god. And that their religion is the only true religion."

"Are you sure," said Alaine. "From what Abbot Keith was saying was that his God is the God above all."

"Which is to say, they believe their God to be superior to ours. It is one thing state you have your own God. It is a whole other thing to say that your own God is superior. Really, we may as well fight if you would claim that."

Alaine, hearing the tone in the queen in the voice, Alaine struggled to find the right words.

"But, but my queen they seem like they mean well."

"Alaine, I am going to tell you this. If a stranger comes to your island thinking that his god is more powerful than yours than you should be very careful. It could very well be a challenge."

With that the conversation ended. Alaine's heart sunk. She looked at her mother 's stern expression. Alaine tought about saying more but fear kept her mouth shut.

Chapter 6

Afeyna was doing her morning harp playing, enjoying the scenery. She sat outside the castle and enjoyed the scenery. The banquet was going to start in just two days.

"Lord," said Afeyna. "I do feel a bit nervous about the upcoming banquet. I do hope that I do glorify you."

As Afeyna was playing her harp, she was feeling an since of unease. As she was playing her harp, it was as though there was this weight on her heart.

What's going on?

As Afeyna played Rephalah went up to her.

"Rephalah," said Afeyna. "What are you doing here."

"I just woke up and was listening to you sing. I could here you sing. I just decided to check up on you."

"I am doing fine. I was thinking about the banquet."

"You have a bad feeling about it."

"Ever since my conversation with Muchara, I have been thinking about what she said."

Rephalah sat with her.

"You know, Muchara does care you about. She wants the best for you."

"I know. But at the same time I have been thinking about what she told me about her past. Rephalah, has Muchara told you anything about her past."

"No," she didn't. "To be honest she does not really like to talk about it. She hardly *ever* talk about it."

"During the civil war that occured in Illunra, Muchara was involved in a conflict. She was involved in that conflict."

"What!"

"She fought against the queen."

Rephalah was in silence.

"I can see why she does not talk about it much."

"Do you understand why I feel that way? Really if she has been keeping secrets like that what else has she been hiding?"

"Afeyna, I am sure Muchara has her reasons for doing what she does. You know she cares about you. You may deny it but deep inside you know."

Afeyna sighed.

"Really Rephalah, I just feel a bit conflicted. When I first heard about the banquet, I was excited but now, I feel a bit confused. Am I ready for this?"

"Have you prayed about it?"

"Yes, everyday I have prayed. And it seems like I haven't gotten any answer."

"Don't worry. God will make it plain eventually."

♪ ♪ ♭

Alaine was in her room thinking about the banquet. She did not sleep much. She thought about the manuscript that she saw and about the conversation she had with Afeyna.

Is this Jesus real?

The more Alained thought about that night, the stronger her desire to get to know the Lord. Alaine knelt down at her bed.

"Jesus," said Alaine. "I do not know much about you. But I

am entrigued by you. I want to know more about you. I accept you into my heart. Please be my Lord and forgive me."

Alaine at that point felt a peace come over her.

"I feel changed. I have to tell everyone!"

♪ ♪ ♭

Afeyna was all arrayed in her clothing for the banquet. She was in her room with her golden harp. Muchara came in to check up on her.

"How are you feeling?"

"A little nervous. Do you think this is a good idea?"

"Afeyna, you said in your heart that this what you feel led to do. If this is what you feel lead to do then I will with you. My prayers are with you."

"Thank you, Muchara. I do appreciate it. You have been a good friend."

"Thank you, Afeyna."

Rephalah entered the room.

"Are you okay," she said.

"Yes, I am fine."

"Don't worry," said Rephalah. "We have been praying for you. You will be fine."

"Thank you all. You have been great to me."

♪ ♪ ♭

The king was in the banquet with his chiefs waiting for Afeyna. The king has been bragging to the chiefs how beautiful she is.

"I have been hearing across the region," said a chief with a grey beard and a scar on his forehead "of the beauty of this Afeyna. They say she has hair that is as hot as the fire of the sun."

"What i often hear is that Afeyna has eyes that are greener the forests of Clehria," said a chief. "And that her skin is as white as teeth."

"Don't worry," said the king. "You chiefs will all get to see Afeyna in her glory. My queen."

"Yes, milord," said the queen as she went up to the king

"Is she ready yet?"

"Almost. I will go check up on her.

♪ ♪ ♭

Afeyna was in the dressing room with Muchara and Rephalah. When the queen walked in and saw Afeyna she paused for moment. Muchara chuckled a bit at the queen's expression.

It looks like even the queen can still be surprised.

"Do you like the look," said Afeyna.

"I must say I am impressed," said the queen. "The chiefs will be all the more impressed."

"You really mean it?"

"Do you think I would lie? Now tell me are you ready?"

"Yes."

"Then come. The king and his chiefs await."

♪ ♪ ♭

The king and the chiefs were sitting the banqueting hall talking. They were immediately silent as Afeyna walked into the room with a Muchara and Rephalah dressed in white. Afeyna with her bright red hair decorated with golden hairpieces and her beautiful green gown looked liked like the queen of forest fairies, and Rephalah and Muchara with their white gowns looked like servants of the fairy queen. However, the two older

79

women might as well has been decorations or worst, invisible as Afeyna was the main show.

The chiefs looked at Afeyna. As Afeyna took out her harp she said the chiefs,

"Hello, my king. And chiefs of Rolunda. I am honored to be here to play for you. Are you ready hear my song."

The king and his chiefs roared. Afeyna began to play her tune.

♪ ♪ ♭

Alaine brought the basket of wine. As she passed the room she heard a conversation. It was Elsiu and her mother.

♪ ♪ ♭

The queen was alone with Elsiu.

"It would appear the time has just about come," said Ereigh.

"Yes," said Elsiu. "But when will Afeyna be dealt with?"

"We don't want to do it too soon," said Ereigh. "Let's wait until the chiefs are drunk. And then we will make our move."

♪ ♪ ♭

Alaine lost her breath as she clenched her basket.

Is mother going to kill Afeyna? What I am going to do?

Afeyna jumped as the queen opened the door.

"Mother."

"Alaine, are you okay?"

"Yes, the wine is finished. I was just taking it to the king and chiefs."

Alaine was about to leave, but she jumped again when the queen called her.

"Alaine."

"Yes, mother."

The queen walked up to her and straightened her hair. Alaine stiffened a little.

"You seem a bit nervous Alaine."

"I am fine, mother. It's that don't go to too many banquets."

"You have nothing to worry. You are lovely girl. You have nothing to worry about. Be yourself."

"Yes, mother."

"You are a lovely girl. You will make someone a good queen."

"Thank you, mother."

Alaine walked off, though, not too fast. It is important to not to get suspicious. When Alaine was out of sight Elsiu walked up to the queen.

"Do you think she knows," said Elsiu.

"I know so," said the queen.

"What should we do to stop her?"

"You don't need to worry. We will not intervene."

"How can you be sure?"

"Tell me, Elsiu. Am I ever wrong?"

"No, my queen. My apologies for doubting you."

"Come let's see how Afeyna is doing."

♪ ♪ ♭

As Afeyna played her harp the kings and chiefs were getting drunk. Afeyna didn't play her harp, something just didn't seem right. The audience was not praising God as they did before. As Muchara sung with Afeyna she began to stop.

"Afeyna …" said Muchara. "This is not glorifying to God."

"Yes," said Rephalah. "This just does not seem right."

"I know," said Afeyna.

When Afeyna stopped the chiefs were wondering why she stopped.

"Why did you stop," said the king. "Come on, continue."

"My king," said Afeyna. "I cannot continue. This does not glorify God."

"Continue!" yelled the king. "Come on! Sing!"

The chiefs all continued to yell.

"Sing!"

Alain as she took to the wine to the king, asked to the king to calm down.

"Quiet! Pour me the wine."

Alaine watching the king, in his angry, drunken stupor simply put the wine down and left. The king cursed her daughter. Afeyna, seeing this, threw the golden harp to the ground.

The king looked at Afeyna.

"What are you doing?"

"I can't do this anymore."

"You would disrespect me in front of my chiefs!"

"I cannot dishonor my God."

"Afeyna..if you do not play that harp. You will be dealt with harshly."

"I … I cannot."

The king looked at Afeyna furiously.

"I give you the honor of playing before me, and this is how you repay me?"

Alaine ran in front of Afeyna.

"Please father," said Alaine. "Don't do this. Please do not be angry with her."

"Alaine!" said the king. "You would rise up against me?"

"No, father! Not at all!"

The queen entered the banquet.

"I must say, Alaine, I am disappointed you would side against your own father."

"Mother!"

The queen looked at the harp that Afeyna threw to the ground.

"I must say, Afeyna," said the queen "I am very disappointed in you. I did not think that you would be so ungrateful. I gave you the best clothing and I gave to you the best harp and this is how you act."

"Listen!" said Muchara. "Afeyna has shown gratefulness to you. She has shown nothing but honor."

"But she shows dishonour by doing this."

The queen pointed to the harp on the floor.

"She must honor God before men," said Muchara.

"If her god did not want her playing before the king then why didn't she say so. She could've spared the king dishonor."

"I am sorry," said Afeyna. "I did not mean dishonor. But this just didn't seem right."

"This will not go unpunished," said the king. "This will be dealt with swiftly. Guards!"

Muchara looked at the queen.

"You planned this didn't you!" she said the queen

"What do you mean?" said the queen

"You have had it out for Afeyna a long time. Or should I say *me*."

"I am not sure you mean..Ebinica."

Muchara struck the queen on the face.

"Run, Afeyna," said Muchara. "RUN! And don't come back."

The queen struck Muchara and Afeyna begun to rip off a portion of her dress and jumped out the window. The guards came, and when they saw Muchara fighting against the queen and one the guards was getting ready to throw a spear at Muchara but Rephalah pushed Muchara away. Rephalah was hit by the spear.

"Rephalah!"

"Take this woman!" said the queen. "And I want her alive."

"Mother!" said Alaine.

Muchara looked at Alaine and shook her head at her.

"Alaine! Go to your room! We will talk later. Guards take her away!"

Alaine watched as the guards took Muchara away. Rephalah was on the ground the wounded. Alaine went up to her .

"Please!" said Muchara. "Do what you will with me, but get help for Rephalah."

"Mother!" said Alaine. "She needs help."

"I said go to your room, Alaine."

Alaine looked at Rephalah.

"Alaine! GO TO YOUR ROOM," said the queen.

Alaine got up and left and she did not look at Rephalah. As Muchara was taken away by the guards, she looked at Rephalah lying on the floor and then she saw the queen look at her with a victorious smile on her face.

I will make you pay for this! You destroyed my friends. And so I will destroy you!

Chapter 7

"Abbot. So this how you honor me."

"My king," said the Abbot. "Afeyna simply wanted to honor God."

The Abbot, the next day stood before the king in the throne room. The queen stood beside the king. The Abbot's monks were with him. Muchara was with them in chains.

"I have given you the honor of standing before me and I allowed Afeyna to play before me. And this is how I am repayed."

"All I can say, my king, is that if Afeyna felt she was honoring God in what she done, then I cannot say anything about her," said Abbot Keith.

The king sighed aggressively.

"Abbot. I could kill you for this. You worked with Ebinica, all this time. For that you should be punished …"

"Please," said Muchara. "St. Keith did not know about my identity. Let him go."

"Quiet Ebinica!" said the king. "I have little reason to believe you. Honestly, I am surprised you decided to come back."

"It was not her choice to come back," said St. Keith. "I felt led to come here. Muchara had her reservations but I wanted to come here."

"Tell me," said the king. "What are your intentions. What are you trying to do."

"I only want to share the share the love of Christ with others. That is my only desire for you, my king."

"Tell me, Abbot," said the king. "Have you came here on behalf your Lord so that you can report back to him, and have him come back to conquer us. Is that it?"

"No, my king. My Lord's kingdom is not of this world."

"Then what is it your lord wants?"

"Your heart."

"Therefore by gaining my heart. He gains my kingdom."

"You see," said the queen. "It is clear what Ebinica's desire is. She knew she couldn't just conquer our kingdom. So she decided to come back with a different plan. After all why try to conquer directly. Ebinica decided to use the monks to conquer in different way."

"Lies!" said Muchara.

The queen continued.

"That different way is a message. And the king accepts this message, he can have the whole kingdom."

"Indeed," said the king. "You are quite clever, Ebinica. But really you should have stayed where you were in the wilderness of Enali."

"Please … king," said Muchara. "The abbot did not all know of my identity. He should not be punished because of me!"

"The abbot and the monks have as much to do with this as you do. And also you assulted my wife so I shall not let this stand."

"Yes, and Rephalah payed for it with her life."

"Her blood will not be satisfactory," said the queen. "It

is *your* blood that I want. Really, I am glad you came back. Because now we can finish what was started."

"We really need to decide on what your sentence will be," said the king.

"Indeed," said the queen. "And sense this is an old friend we will should find something suitable."

"That sounds like a plan," said the king. "But for now we shall hold them in prison until we can finally decide their punishment."

♪ ♩ ♭

Muchara sat alone in prison with the monks. She was shackled to the wall.

"I am sorry, Muchara," said the abbot. "It was not my desire that we would end up here."

"You have nothing to apologize for, Abbot. It is my fault you are here. I should've just stayed away and then you would have been safe."

"Muchara," said St. Keith. "When I chose to do this. I understood the risks. If going to the castle meant the risk of emprisonment, it was a risk I was willing to take."

"You are a brave monk," said Muchara. "That is why I admire you."

"I believe in following my Lord regardless of whatever the cost may be. He bled and died for me on a cross, so I can handle a prison."

"Abbot," said Muchara. "I would like to say that no matter what happens, I am happy to have served with you."

"I as well," said St. Keith.

While in prison, St. Keith began singing hymns and thanking the Lord. The monks joined him in singing. Muchara sung with the monks. She could see the joy on their faces as she sung with them.

Everything will be fine

♪ ♪ ♭

The next day, one of the guards came to their cell.

"All right abbot, you're coming with us."

Muchara and the guards watched as the guards took the abbot away. Muchara shouted for the abbot. But Abbot Keith told her,

"Take heart," said St. Keith. "We have have already overcome the world."

The guards took St. Keith away. Muchara waited for what seemed like forever.

"Oh, Lord," said Muchara. "Please be with St. Keith."

Muchara and the monks began to pray.

Later on that night, Alaine came to their cell.

"Alaine," said Muchara. "What are you doing here?"

"I have come to get you out."

"Why. Muchara … they killed St. Keith."

"That can't be!"

"It … is true. That is why I had to come set you free. Because you are next."

"Alaine …" said Muchara. "I cannot have you risking your life for me. If the queen knew …"

"I shall fear no man or woman," said Alaine. "The Lord is with me."

Alaine opened the door.

"Come, she said I help you escape."

"We will stay," said the monks. "We will be fine."

Alaine led Muchara out of the castle. Muchara thanked

Alaine. As Muchara left, she looked at the castle with an angry expression.

Abbot Keith, Rephalah, you will all be avenged.

"And 'Queen' Ereigh, when I come back, it will be army. I promise you that! Ebinica has returned."

Muchara left the castle now ready for war.

Printed in the United States
by Baker & Taylor Publisher Services